The Price of Fame

The Price of Fame

Nneka Bilal

THE PRICE OF FAME

iUniverse books may be ordered through booksellers or by contacting:

iUniverse
1663 Liberty Drive
Bloomington, IN 47403
www.iuniverse.com
1-800-Authors (1-800-288-4677)

Because of the dynamic nature of the Internet, any web addresses or links contained in this book may have changed since publication and may no longer be valid. The views expressed in this work are solely those of the author and do not necessarily reflect the views of the publisher, and the publisher hereby disclaims any responsibility for them.

Any people depicted in stock imagery provided by Thinkstock are models, and such images are being used for illustrative purposes only. Certain stock imagery © Thinkstock.

ISBN: 978-1-5320-0580-0 (sc)
ISBN: 978-1-5320-0581-7 (e)

Print information available on the last page.

iUniverse rev. date: 09/08/2016

ONE

Ebony twirled the thorny stem between her thumb and index finger, pricking her skin with every rotation. Little red blood bubbles formed but she felt no pain. Her fingers rubbed the red silky petals remembering the first time she had felt the flower; the shaky hand of a sixteen year old boy meeting his future father in law for the first time as he picked up his date for the spring dance. He slipped the red rose corsage on her wrist kissing her hand. The couple left the house hand in hand with the watchful eye of her father.

The petals tickled her nose remembering a happy time in her life, her heart in pieces thinking how to live without the man that she had loved for a lifetime. The tears ran to the tip of her nose before getting caught up by a tissue. Her mother sat to her left in a long black dress motionless. The dark shades sat on her face with tears running from under them. Her sister on her right with her face covered with a black lace veil. Ebony's feet support her shaky body as she rose walking over to the casket. She picked a yellow tulip from the huge bouquet that sat to the left of the casket peeling the petals slowly letting them flutter over her father's casket. Her knees buckle. The cool, spiky grass comforted her head as the casket is lowered into the ground. A warm hand touches her shoulder before scooping her up and carrying her back to her seat.

"I got you baby." The strong hands place her on his lap hugging her tightly. She falls into her husband's chest letting all her pain out. Carson grabs his wife tightly rocking her like a child. At that moment, Ebony was so thankful that this man had stood by her through their turbulent year last year and all her betrayal with his ex friend Jefferson. Her head lifts up and stares at the coffin again secretly saying one last goodbye to her father. She wiped her hand over her husband's tear soaked shirt hoping the stain would come out. Her face turned to her mother and she knew that she had to find strength from somewhere if not for any one else, for her mother. She slid off of Carson's lap taking her mother into her arms as she collapsed like a baby into her daughter. The memory of her father's heart attack and him being rushed to the hospital all played back in her mind. The pit of her stomach had an awful ache in it. How can she possibly go on without her father's guidance, strength, and protection?

After the burial, the family received guests at the house. Mrs. Lovely had hired a caterer to take the stress of her. Ebony watched her mother wear a fake smile as everyone gave their condolences, while she sat in her father's favorite green corduroy fabric chair motionless. She put her face into the fabric inhaling the musty, manly smell her father wore remembering how as a young child she would climb into her fathers lap while he read stories to her. It was the safest place in the world. Everyone danced around her as she was paralyzed by her thoughts. Her worst nightmare would be that all the commotion in her life caused her father stress and a heart attack. She starred out the window that showed their front porch, thinking of how many times her and her father have sat out there swinging together as she talked about her dreams with him.

"How you holding up sweetie?" Her best friend kneeled in front of her touching her knee.

"I'm okay and you? I know my dad was a second father to you."

"He was the only father I knew." Melody's eyes swelled up with water. Her father had left their family at a young age which made the Lovely household her second home.

"Maybe I should cancel our honeymoon?" Ebony looked to her mom and younger sister.

"I think you need to get away. It will be good for you to clear your head and come back strong for your family."

"And for you? I do have to get you down the aisle in two weeks."

The two friends hugged each other for support. Carson shot his wife a wink from across the room and Ebony watched India run out of the house in a short skirt and three inch heels. Her eye brows lowered wondering what would be so important for her sister to leave her own father's funeral.

TWO

⟨⟐⟩

The sun peeked through the blinds warming Ebony's swollen face. She peeled her face off the tear soaked pillow case. Looking at the mascara on her white case reminded her of her sleepless night and the reality that she had just buried her father the day before. She rolled over onto her husband chest. His arm circled her back comforting her. Carson looked down on her before kissing her forehead. She looked up to meet his eyes.

"Good morning sweetheart."

She gave him a half smile, not in the mood to talk. Her husband rubbed his hand over her hair like her father use to do when he tucked her in bed at night. She closed her eyes placing her hand over her heart. The pain was unbearable. She thought of all the nights her and her father would sit on the porch swing talking into the early morning. She needed to hear him tell her no dream was too big for her to reach one last time. Her father was the only one who was always on her side. Her mother always judged her but her dad would just hug her giving a reassuring smile.

Ebony rolled to the side out of her husband's reach letting Carson's hand fall to the bed sheets. She walked to the dresser mirror looking at her red eyes. She rubbed them causing more moisture.

"What can I do?" Her husband swung his feet to the floor coming behind his wife. His right hand moved the loose hair from her neck making room for his lips to kiss it. "I want to help you through this." Her half smile appeared again in her reflection in the mirror. The corners of her brown eyes drooped.

"I just need time." She made a u-turn leaving her husband's lips poked out. Ebony climbed her limp body back into the bed pulling the sheets over her head.

....

Carson's lips kissed his wife on the forehead as she opened her eyes.

"Are you going to get up today? I think you should check on your mother." He spoke softly. "I know you lost your father, but she did lose her husband."

His wife turned her nose up at him before putting her pillow over her head. She was not ready to get out of her own depression to help someone else out of theirs. Yes it was selfish, but she was not in the right mind to think straight.

"I'm worried about you baby." She heard her husband's muffled voice. The reality was she was the older sister and should be taking care of her sister and mother right now. Ebony removed the pillow from her face to find her husband starring at her.

She threw the pillow at him before rolling out the bed. Dragging herself to the bathroom, she took a shower that was two days past due. Ebony threw on a pair of jeans, a pale pink button up shirt and a pair of tennis shoes to go visit her mother. She parked her Honda Accord on the street walking up the short driveway. Ebony let herself in with her key but then thought maybe she should have knocked. The house was quiet, no television, no radio, and no noise at all.

"Mom?" She hollered out in the foyer trying to determine which direction to go in. Her mother said nothing. Ebony headed up the steps to her parent's room. She drew back the blinds to let some light in the closed up room. The bed was untouched. She peeked into the bathroom; still nothing. She made her way down the hallway where her sister's and her childhood bedrooms were. All the doors were closed which was unusual. Ebony opened the first door which was her old room. The smell of alcohol almost knocked her out. A female body lay curled up on the bed in a pair of black yoga pants and a white t-shirt. She took a few small steps forward, her breath trapped in her throat. The image of her father lying in the casket flashed in her brain. A chill ran down her spine to the tips of her finger tips that were shaking on their own. Her mother made a loud grunting noise bringing the life back into her body. Ebony backed out of the room shutting the door quietly. Her knees buckled. Water droplets ran from her eyes as her reality set in. The thought of losing both parents would be overwhelming. She curled her body in a ball hugging her knees tightly. This was supposed to be the happiest times of her life. Her best friend getting married in a few days, her marriage back on track after that whole cheating fiasco last year, and the career she had always wanted was coming together, but without her father to share it with, nothing felt right and her mother was having a very hard time. Ebony thought maybe she should go back to work with her mother to help her get through the next few months, but that would be putting her new music career on hold.

"Thud". She lifted her head as the noise came from down the hall. Her face dried up quickly as she jumped to her feet following the sound she had just heard. Opening the second bedroom door, which was her sister's old room, she found her lying on the floor.

"What is going on today?" She said out loud as she entered the room.

The curtains were shut with only a small rectangle of light coming in. The room looked like her sister never moved out. Clothes covering the tan carpet, the bed never made, and the stench of sweat and alcohol filled the air. Ebony marched right up to the twin bed, taking a seat on it and kicking her sister with the tip of her toe.

"Get up." She yelled at her.

"What bitch?" India rolled over opening her eyes to focus on her sister.

"What is going on? You're passed out, mom's passed out. What are you doing here?"

"I had a gig out here and couldn't make it back to the city, mom." Her sarcasm poured out of her lips.

India slowly pulled herself to a sitting position. She rubbed her forehead.

"What kind of gig? What is going on with you?" Ebony stood reaching her hand out to help pull her younger sister off the floor. India knocked her sister back onto the bed once she was on her feet as she made a mad dash to the bathroom. Ebony rushed after her then backed out quickly as her sister lost what looked like everything she had eaten the previous day.

"Oh yuck."

Ebony went downstairs to the kitchen to make her mother and sister some tea. The always tidy kitchen held a sink full of dirty dishes, pizza boxes spread out on the wooden kitchen table, and a family of ants parading around the window sill. Ebony opened the flowered mini curtain letting the sunlight bounce off the coral walls.

Thirty minutes later the kitchen was clean and ant free. She took her tea cup into the living room curling up in her father's old recliner. All the good memories of her childhood home with her dad flooded her mind again added to the worry of her mother and sister. How was she going to help her family get through this when she missed her father just as much as they did? The only difference was she had her husband to keep her company and her mind focused on other things. The two hung over women dragged themselves into the kitchen.

"Well good afternoon." Ebony put on a fake smile. "There's some tea."

She watched her mother pour a cup of tea and they joined her in the living room on the old brown sofa that they use to curl up on and have movie nights when they were kids. The three women sat in silence starring at the television like it was on. India's eyes were heavy with her natural hair sticking out of the top of a bright yellow bandana. Her mother looked beat, like she hadn't had a good night sleep in months which was probably fact. She sat motionless holding her cup of tea with two hands starring at a small spot on the carpet or nothing at all.

"Mom?" Ebony said quietly.

Nothing. Her head slowly lifted, blood shot eyes meeting her daughter's eyes.

"I'm fine… I'm fine." She shouted. Ebony's eyes grew big but her sister didn't react at all. Ebony shifted in her seat wanting to get up, run out the house and never look back but Carson's face popped into her head knowing he would be disappointed for not trying to connect with them.

"Mom." She started again slowly.

"I…" Her voice was low and dark. "I just want some time to honor the man that I have loved for thirty-five years. Is that too much to ask?" Her mother stood walking towards Ebony. "Is it?" She raised her voice. Ebony's eyes widened. She had never heard her mother raise her voice like that before. Not even when Ebony came home with a D in English her freshman year of high school.

"Mom."

"I just want my husband back, my life back, and my world to be normal again." Ebony's eyes burned as the tears filled them. Her heart hurt watching her mother crumble in front of her. She had never seen her so vulnerable and she wanted her father back as much as her mother did. Ebony stood to her feet extending her arms to comfort her mother. For the first time her mother was not the strong, stern woman that she had always known. She seemed helpless and lost and Ebony had no idea how to be there for her so she took a step forward and grabbed her mother as tightly as she could.

THREE

*C*arson pulled up to the gym happy to be out of his dreary house. He loved his wife dearly, but lately he hasn't been able to reach her. She has been distant and didn't even get out of bed most days. The death of his father in law crushed his wife and he had to find a way to get her through this.

He spotted his boy's BMW a few spots over. He took a deep breath needing some male company.

"I haven't seen you in weeks." Mike commented as Carson dropped his bag in the locker room.

"I know. The death of my father in law has been real hard on Ebony. I feel I can't leave her alone."

"Is she suicidal?" Carson rolled his eyes.

"She's pushing me away." Carson puts on his weight lifting gloves. "I just need to relieve some stress."

"Then we should be at a strip club with some titties in our faces."

"You will never change." Michael chuckled as they stopped at a weight bench extending his arm for Carson to take the first set.

"You know I really want to do something special for my wife. I was thinking a late honeymoon or something. You know of any places within budget?"

"No offense man, but you are real cheap."

The two men switched places.

"No, I am sensible."

"If you say so. What about the Poconos or somewhere local?"

"We could do the mountains. I just hope she gets out of the bed to come with me."

"She will. For some reason she loves your cheap ass." Michael said as he pushed up on the weights. Carson's eyes followed a pair of shapely legs walking through the gym. He couldn't see her face but she had a nice round ass that jiggled in her tight work out pants.

"Yo! Are you going to spot me?"

"Oh I'm sorry." Carson snapped back to reality. Michael sat up from the bar.

"What are you looking at?"

"I thought I saw Leslie." Michael chuckled.

"Her crazy ass is locked up. You don't have to worry about her."

"I guess." Carson said as he looked for the woman who had seemed to disappear into thin air. After all the drama she caused last year, he definitely did not want to see her.

FOUR

———— ⌦ ————

"I quit." Ebony put her white apron down on the counter with a grin that made her face ache. After receiving a small advance check from the record label, the thought of waiting another table irritated her. It wasn't much money, but her husband had promised to take care of all the bills for a little. She looked at her boss who had been nothing but good to her, but the reality of her new life was overwhelming her with joy and she had always dreamt of making a big dramatic exit.

"Don't forget about us when you are rich and famous." One of her co workers said. It felt good to smile since she hadn't seen one in weeks but she knew her dad wouldn't want her to sulk and he definitely didn't want her waiting tables anymore.

As she walked to her car, she passed the alley way where Jefferson had trapped her and pleasured her body by the dumpster. Her body trembled remembering the feeling of his tongue in places that her husband had never reached.

"Those thoughts need to go away." She told herself as she climbed into her Honda Accord headed to the dress shop to meet Melody for their final fitting. Ebony ran into the dress shop fashionably late. She stopped mid stride as she spotted her best friend in the three way mirror looking like a ghetto princess. Melody spotted her in the mirror turning to face her. Ebony wiped her eyes so proud of her best friend for making this commitment, but not sure that she could actually keep it.

"Wow, you look incredible. And the fit is perfect." Melody twirled in her dress.

"Just loose that bright nail polish, the rollers, and that weave. Why did you come out the house in rollers, you know better than that." The two friends laugh.

"I have a date tonight with Keith so you know how it is."

Ebony shook her head because she didn't.

"The alterations look great." The seamstress pulled at the dress making sure all the pins were out and the dress was perfect.

"You have no give in this dress so you better not breath wrong in it or else."

"I know right." Melody laughed as she retreated back into the dressing room to take the dress off. Ebony walked around the shop looking at all the new dresses on the models. Part of her wished she was doing it all over again just to try on the dresses.

"I would definitely get this one if I did it all over again." Melody looked at her best friend sideways as she walked up to her in her jeans and blouse. "Not that I would, I'm just saying."

"Ok, you had me worried for a second."

"No my marriage is in tact. No worries here. In fact, Carson is taking me on a mini honeymoon but I will be back before the wedding of course."

"Thank you." Ebony said as they took two glasses of Champaign from one of the workers at the shop. Melody and Ebony took a seat while they waited for the dress to be steamed.

"As much as this dress cost they should have given us the whole bottle."

"So how are you? I haven't seen you since..." Melody's voice trailed off knowing that the last time they saw each other Ebony was burying her father.

"I've been better but I'm getting there. I'm sorry; I know my dad was supposed to walk you down the aisle."

Melody wiped her right eye. Mr. Lovely had been a second father to her since she didn't really know her real father so his death was hard on her as well.

"Yeah, this hasn't been easy on any of us." Ebony grabbed her best friend's hand as they sat in silence reminiscing.

"You're all set ma'am." The sales associate said carrying the long dress bag. Ebony took it from the lady.

"I'll see you when I get back." Ebony hugged her best friend tightly before they went their separate ways.

His wife pulled into the driveway. Carson looked down at his watch. He had wanted to be on the road by now. The timing was off and he knew it with the wedding and her new job as a singer things were hectic but he knew his wife needed this time away to clear her head and the two of them needed to reconnect emotionally and hopefully sexually.

"Let me hang up her dress and I will be ready." Ebony ran into the house to hang Melody's dress up. Her bags were already in the car. She returned climbing into the passenger seat. Carson took the drivers seat adjusting his rear view mirror.

"You have everything?" He turned to his wife who was buckling her seat belt.

"I am so glad we are doing this." Carson's face lit up with delight. Ebony smiled, happy to see her husband so happy and hoping that the time away will help her with her father's death. She had stayed in bed for three long weeks and her husband finally persuaded her to leave town with him. Her marriage needed to be a priority. The guilt of last year was still weighing on her since she was the one who cheated.

As the car made its way up the mountains, Ebony starred out the window admiring the beautiful colors. Her father loved long car rides and the fall. As a kid they use to travel during their summer break. The whole family playing the license plate game or I spy as they drove across the country. Ebony's eyes watered. Her husband reached over rubbing his hand over her hair pulling out her pony tail holder.

"You ok over there?" Her husband asked. Ebony shook her head wiping her nose and turning back to the window. She shifted in her seat pulling off her shoes to cross her legs in the seat. She glanced at her husband who had a smile plastered across his face. She would have to pull herself together somehow for the sake of her husband who was so excited about this trip. She appreciated his effort.

"I am truly happy. All that craziness is behind us and we can focus on us again." Carson rambled on grabbing his wife's face making her lips poke out as he kissed them gently after he parked in front of the resort. She watched her husband get out of the car to get their room key. She hoped Carson splurged a little to get one of those fancy rooms with the champagne glasses in the middle of the floor.

"You ready for a great weekend?" Carson hopped back into the car driving up a windy path to a row of secluded rooms. He opened the room door, scooped up his wife carrying her into the room. Ebony's face dropped. There was no champagne glass like on the brochure, but she saw a pink, heart shaped hot tub and red heart shaped bed with mirrors all over the ceiling.

"This is either romantic or real tacky." Ebony said out loud by accident.

"You don't like it." She rolled out of his arms steadying her feet on the floor.

"No, I do I do. I'm glad that you planned this." She forced a smile.

The moon had risen over the mountain tops and Ebony felt tired after the drive. A hot dinner, a warm bath, and a good night sleep were all she could think about. Carson ran around the room like a little kid, exploring every inch of it. She had to admit that it was kind of romantic, but a romantic villa in the Caribbean with a private butler was more of what she was looking for.

"Come" Carson patted the empty space next to him as he finally settled on the red, heart shaped bed. Something had told her to pack her own sheets and a bottle of Lysol. She obliged. The couple lay back on the bed starring at each other through the ceiling mirrors. Her husband closed his eyes looking so peaceful. She rolled onto her side in his air space.

"Are you really happy with me?"

His eyes opened wide, pupils moving quickly back and forth like he was searching for some type of truth in her eyes.

"Are you?" His chest rose as he inhaled.

"Of course I am." Her eye twitched slightly. His lips landed on the tip of her nose as he exhaled.

"I have loved you for three decades." Ebony's lips turned up at the thought of having one man's true love. She kissed him gently on his lips. Carson rolled over climbing on top of his wife. He kissed her again deeper brushing his hand across her temple. Ebony unbuttoned his jeans pulling them down then she removed her own pants. Carson mounted her. Ebony stared at his naked butt in the mirror as it moved up and down. She closed her eyes trying to focus on the moment, but her thoughts wanted him to flip her over, smack her ass and pleasure her body until she couldn't take it any more; the way Jefferson use to do.

"Stop it" Ebony said to her thoughts.

"Stop what?"

"Not you baby, I'm sorry." Carson rolled his eyes and kept moving until he found his climax a few minutes later.

The couple lay naked spooning each other. Ebony's fingers dragged across her husband's arm. Visions of the last year kept her from sleeping. Carson seemed very forgiving after her affair with Jefferson which she was a little surprised about, grateful but surprised. Her fear is that the man that always liked to be in control and pinch a penny will not be able to live with a wife who is successful and makes more money than him. Ebony likes to splurge, but Carson wants his money to sit in a bank account and build for emergencies. Carson had always accepted his wife with all her flaws. He was everything she wasn't and that brought them together, but sometimes his sweet love making wasn't enough. Ebony squeezed her high school sweet heart tightly, loving him for so many years, but is love always enough to keep people together?

The sun peaked through the drapes as Ebony's eye lids got heavy.

"Rise and shine." Carson drew the blinds letting the sunlight flush into the room. Her eyes focused in on a silver dining cart with a single red rose in a tall clear vase.

"That smells delicious. I'm starving." She sat upright looking into the covered dishes.

"I got your favorite, pancakes." Her face lit up.

"You always take care of me."

Over the next two days, the Brody's enjoyed horseback riding through the mountains, long hikes through the woods, and a quiet picnic on the edge of a cliff with a bottle of homemade wine.

"This is beautiful." Ebony commented starring out as the sun started to tuck behind the mountains. The sky was layered with blends of reds, oranges, blues and purple. She leaned into her husband as he put his arm around her.

"It truly is."

"Out here with nothing, it makes you think anything is possible. I feel all my dreams are about to come true."

Ebony smiled thinking of her exciting singing career that she hoped was about to happen. Her face cracked and the tears streamed down her face. She hugged her knees tightly biting the top of her knee.

"I miss my dad." Her head dropped between her legs as her husband caressed her back.

"I know baby, I know."

FIVE

"He needs a bad girl." India sang out shaking her booty like she was one of Beyonce's back up dancers.

"Where did your sister learn those moves?" Melody asked her best friend.

"It makes you wonder huh?" Ebony took a big gulp from her wine glass wondering what her sister had been up to living in that big city alone.

"So we are playing it safe this time?" Melody laughed at her best friend probably thinking of the escapades that followed her friend's bachelorette party last year.

"Yes we are, but I still planned a great night." She handed her a glass of Moet before joining the thirteen other ladies that were occupying the living room. She had sent her husband away for the evening to have the house to their selves.

"Let's start this party." Ebony turned the knob up on the radio. It felt like Usher was in the room with them. India jumped up and fell into a split onto the floor as her natural hair never moved out of place.

"Where did you learn that? Melody asked in awe. I need to learn that for my wedding night. Keith will be very happy."

Ebony shook her head as she finished her third glass of wine. The one good thing about her impromptu honeymoon was that she had brought back a whole bunch of homemade wine from the mountains. Her and Carson had to get back for the wedding which was tomorrow so she didn't have much time to plan her best friend's bachelorette party which should have been last week but everything seemed to be working out.

A knock came from the door as she headed to refill her glass. Ebony opened it starring two male police officers in the face. One stood about 6 feet, chocolate and bald head. The other was a few inches shorted with dreadlocks and the same smooth brown skin. She backed up from the door allowing them to enter the house.

"Turn off that music!" The brown skinned officer with the dreads bellowed out.

"You ladies are making too much noise and it looks like some underage drinking going on." His flashlight scanned the crowd of women. His long black shiny shoes stopped in front of Melody flashing the light down her low cut blouse.

"You see something you like officer?" She smiled devilishly. Leave it to her to flirt with a cop. Grabbing her right arm, he swung her around causing her glass of wine to fall shattering on the wooden floor. He stretched her arms on the wall spreading her legs as wide as her skirt would allow. Her arms no longer free as he binds them with handcuffs. Melody poked her butt up, shaking it, begging to be punished. Ebony laughed because she knew her best friend was too smart for her to trick. The other officer pulled his hat off letting his bald head breathe. He positioned his body in front of her best friend, scooping her off the ground. She wrapped her legs tightly around his waist for support showing all her goodies as her skirt rose to her waist. Ebony covered her mouth embarrassed for her best friend who did not seem to mind that the whole room was starring at her leopard print thong underwear.

"Turn that music up." Melody yelled.

The music came on and the two dancers went wild smacking every ass in sight. Ebony backed up into the corner finding an empty chair thinking of the last time she saw strippers and the strain on her relationship that followed that night. She worried for Melody who was more promiscuous than she. Her eyes focused on her best friend whose lips were attached to one of the officers. Ebony reached for an open bottle of wine sitting on the end table next to her. She laughed to herself thinking Carson would have a fit if he could see the state of their living room right now. Melody stumbled over to her best friend, freeing herself from the officer's lips.

"I think your sister was a stripper in her former life." Ebony looked at her sister who was bouncing her ass on the floor again.

"Yeah" She said half dazed. Ebony squinted. Her sister left her father's funeral early, has been drunk lately, and now having the time of her life dancing like a stripper and acting very out of character. What was really going on with her? Their relationship has had a strain since last year and she knew her sister would not trust in her to tell her the truth. She had to find some way to connect with her which was always her father's job.

"What's wrong?" Melody asked.

"This whole scene just brings back the start of some bad memories." The two friends touch hands.

"But that is all behind you now. You and Carson are stronger than ever and your about to blow up." Melody jumped up exploding out of her chair. Ebony giggled feeling her alcohol and laughing at her friend who still had handcuffs dangling from her wrist.

"Are you sure you're ready to get married?"

She frowns. "Why would you ask me that?"

"I know you love sex and with different people and marriage changes all that." Ebony's mind took her to a time when she was having great sex, just not with her husband. She smirked.

"Don't go there." Her best friend's finger waved in her face.

"What?"

"You're thinking of him."

"No I'm not." Her eye twitched. "He tried to ruin my life and my marriage, remember?"

"And then we found out it was his sister, remember?"

Melody got up and joined officer dread head in a strip tease.

Ebony tucked her legs under her body. Her face went from happy to sad, frustration, anger, and desire as she thought of the two men that invaded her life. Melody was right. Jefferson had tricked her at first but then she fell for him and he opened her eyes to so many things and once they found out Leslie was behind everything she couldn't hate him anymore and the truth of the matter was that Jefferson didn't make her cheat but the things he did to her kept her cheating. She was missing that spark in her marriage that drove her to do it. Words to a song popped in her head. She jotted the words down before she forgot them. Giggling from excitement to go to the studio next week to lay some tracks down, her life felt surreal at that moment.

Melody and India seemed to take over the whole show and turn it into their own strip show. Ebony laughed at them realizing how thankful she was to have them in her life.

....

Carson opened the side door scanning the house. Empty bottles of wine and champagne flooded the kitchen counter, trash can, and living room floor along with five drunken women, one of them his wife. His sister in law was face down on the hard floor exposing a lot of skin. His wife was on the love seat, mouth open snoring very loudly which she only did when she had too much to drink with her feet resting on her best friend who was leaned up right on the couch. He shook his head in disappointment knowing he should have enforced that they get a hotel suite instead of their house. He thought his wife would have been the level headed one in the group, but he was wrong. Grabbing a broom from the pantry he swept up the broken glass that was on his beautiful hard wood floors then picked up the trash and empty bottles filling two trash bags of trash. Once the house looked half way back to normal, he tapped his wife on the cheek to wake her. It was a little past nine am and the wedding was this evening. He felt half way responsible because if they didn't go on their honeymoon then her bachelorette party wouldn't have been so last minute.

"What?" His wife barked opening her eyes.

She smiled as her eyes focused on him. "It's after nine. Don't you have a hair appointment?"

Ebony pulled her body upright looking around the room.

"Oh my." She turned her head. She noticed the clock on the microwave. "OH MY." She shouted.

Ebony kicked her best friend. "Melody get up, we gotta go."

Carson walked to the other women nudging them slightly so they could get out of his house. His wife ran upstairs hopefully to brush her teeth and put a comb through her hair.

"Melody, get up. You're getting married today." Melody opened her eyes looking at him strangely. "Do you know where you are?" He laughed as she stumbled trying to get to her feet. His wife came running down the steps with a pair of wrinkled jeans, a yellow shirt, and a pair of tennis shoes on.

"We gotta go. Our hair appointment was at 9." Ebony grabbed her best friend pulling her towards the door.

"Be careful." He yelled after them. She waved him off.

"What about these people?" He asked as she slammed the door shut.

"Great." He flopped down on an empty spot on the couch. He put his nose to it smelling the stint of alcohol and stale perfume. He looked down at his feet at his sister in law.

Carson woke up India. She would help get these ladies out. The two of them cleared the house within minutes.

"You want some breakfast?" He asked her.

"Sure." India sat on the bar stool putting her head down.

"I'm so dizzy." Carson smiled at her passing her two aspirin. He liking the feeling of being needed; feeling like a man.

SIX

―――――――――――― ⤜⧓⤏ ――――――――――――

"My hands won't stop sweating. Was it like this for you?" Melody waved her hands trying to get them dry. Her best friend smiled at her remembering her wedding day.

"You'll be fine. I think everyone gets nervous."

"Am I doing the right thing?" Melody turned to her best friend with such fear in her eyes. Ebony was so use to seeing her friend in a playful manor, but seeing true fear in her eyes was something very new. She grabbed her friend's hands to steady them.

"You will be fine; just don't ask me for any marriage advice. The two laughed.

"Five minutes ladies." India poked her head into the back room at the church where they were getting dressed.

"We should have gone to Vegas. I know people have lots to say. After all the men I've been with, I feel like a hypocrite wearing white."

Ebony stood behind her best friend as she took one last look in the full length mirror. The off white satin dress trimmed with rhinestones accenting her ample bosom area was tapered to below the knee when the bottom became lace and flowed down past her feet and had a twelve inch train attached. Her rhinestone head band sat in front of her curls that framed her bun. Melody flipped the lace in front of her beautifully done up face.

"Everyone deserves their happily ever after." She squeezed her shoulders. "You look beautiful."

Melody touched her best friend's hand giving her a smile that comforted every fear that she had at that moment.

The door opened again. "It's almost time."

Ebony took one last look in the mirror at her short charcoal satin dress that draped over her left shoulder, grabbed her matron of honor bouquet and headed for the door. Standing at the top of the aisle brought back memories although this time her husband was already beside her. She looked at Carson, reached for his hand, and started their slow walk together.

All the guests rose as Melody started down the aisle. She smiled at her future husband who was dressed in a long tailed white tuxedo with a charcoal vest and bow tie on, walking briskly towards him. Ebony hoped that her friend truly wanted this. She thought of a conversation they shared in high school where Melody had sworn she would never get married because she never wanted the same piece of dick for the rest of her life.

Melody handed her bouquet over as she took Keith's hand. Melody had only known him for a few months, but in that time she had never seen her friend happier or more committed to one person.

Ebony stood looking over the crowd of well dressed people and a chill shot through her body. She tried to shake it off, but a strange feeling came over her like someone was watching her. Her eyes shot to Carson who was focused on the happy couple. Ebony located her sister in the audience who seemed to be texting at the moment. She couldn't help but think how her sister has been different since her father passed. Her eyes searched quickly looking for anything peculiar and in the very back row she spotted a woman dressed in a big black hat that resembled Leslie. She shifted her weight from one foot to the other hoping Carson would catch her movement which he didn't. He was in a daze with the same goofy smile, probably reliving their wedding day in his mind. She focused her attention to the back row again. She tightened her lips and lowered her eye brows. She saw the lady in all black get up from her seat and slip out the door before anyone noticed her. Ebony's leg tapped on the thin carpet which finally caught her husband's attention. He lowered his eye brows and shot her a dirty look from six feet away. Ebony squinted back at him mad that no one else noticed the disturbance and frustrated that the priest was still talking while a crazy lady was in their presence. She was supposed to be locked up somewhere, how Leslie could be free this soon after trying to kill her only a few months ago was beyond reason.

"You may kiss the bride." The priest announced.

"Thank God." Ebony said out loud not realizing it. Her husband lowered his eyes in disproof.

"What is wrong with you?" Carson asked as soon as the wedding party exited the church and came back in to take pictures.

"I think I saw Leslie." He shook his head at her over active imagination. "That is all behind us baby." He kissed her hand pacifying her.

Ebony ignored him knowing what she saw and knowing her husband thinks everyone is good and even when all the craziness with Jefferson happened, he was still quick to forgive.

The flash of the camera blinded the bridal party as they assembled in the church after all the guests had exited.

"Bride and groom only, parents of the groom, females only…" The young, white photographer ordered commands every few minutes. Ebony looked at her best friend who wore a smile but Ebony knew better. Happiness and joy was what she experienced last night with the officers ass in her face. Melody seemed content, but not overjoyed.

The bridal party's three white stretch limos pulled up to the reception hall after forty- five minutes of picture taking. The midnight blue covered room gave the illusion of being under the midnight sky. Tall cream colored candles illuminated the room giving off shadows from the white roses, lilies, and babies breathe reflecting from the tables. Carson reached his hand out to his wife as their dinner plates were being collected. She joined him on the dance floor.

"I'm so glad we can get our life back to normal."

She pulled back looking into his eyes. "But it's not normal. You have stopped playing basketball and with my career, things will not be the same."

"I heard Jefferson left town, so I think we are good." Carson pulled his wife back into him swaying to the music. His hand trailed down her bare back.

"Who told you that?" She inquired. Her heart sank a little thinking of not seeing Jefferson again. The whole fiasco last year was crazy, but she truly connected with that man. He brought out something in her that her husband couldn't.

"Michael did." Ebony rested her head on her husbands shoulder watching as the new couple who was a few feet away held each other tightly as they danced the night away. Ebony watched her best friend with a Barbie doll smile plastered on her face.

"Do you think Melody is really happy?" Carson turned his head in the direction of the couple.

"Why wouldn't she be, she is marrying a rich, good looking guy. That's what's important to her; money, sex, and looks. You two are so different yet so close." His bluntness was shied upon by his wife, but he was right about Melody but his opinion on her was biased.

"I guess so." Ebony looked on wondering if her friend really did marry for the right reasons.

SEVEN

—⊸≋⊷—

"Good morning." Carson's sweaty lips touched the tip of his wife's forehead as he returned from his morning run.

"Since you stopped working, I am a little jealous you get to sleep in."

"You wouldn't sleep in even if you could." Ebony sat up in bed. "And I am working, just not punching a clock." She rubbed her eyes wiping the sleep away. Her husband walked into the bathroom. Her face exploded in excitement thinking of her studio session with Joe later. The steam from the shower filled the bed room as Carson left the door open. Ebony took that as a sign. They hadn't made love since the impromptu trip to the Poconos. Ebony twisted out of bed putting her feet on the carpet. She dropped her nightgown next to the bed. Carson's eyes widened as his wife stepped into the stream of water with him.

"Want some company?" She grabbed the bar of soap from his hand lathering it up in hers, and caressing his back with the suds.

"You want to make love to your wife in the shower?"

"You know I have to get to work." Her lips tickled the back of his ear. She ran her finger nails down his back cupping his butt. Carson jumped slightly.

"You are distracting me. I can't be late today."

His words hit like the cool air hitting her behind from the back of the shower. Ebony's face dropped feeling the rejection from her husband. After all that has happened, she thought that maybe he would break his morning routine but he is a creature of habit and still was. Ebony climbed out of the shower frustrated and hurt. This was not a conversation she wanted to have with her husband because it's a fight not worth fighting. She grabbed her robe from the closet and went down stairs to put on a pot of hot water. As Ebony pulled down a striped coffee mug, she heard a rustling outside the house. The cup slipped out of her hand crashing to the ground. She scurried to the front door, opening it and looking around outside. The mild spring air seeped up under her robe. Ebony grabbed the bottom, closing it before all her goodies were exposed to the whole neighborhood. Stepping back into the house, she saw small white envelope out of the corner of her eye. Scanning the outside, she saw nothing unfamiliar; her elderly neighbor walking the dog, the lady across the street rocking on the front porch with probably her third cup of coffee by now, and her next door neighbor tending to his lawn which was already perfect.

Ebony scooped up the envelope taking it to the kitchen table. Her name was on the front so she opened it.

The Lovely Ebony who gets everything she wants except maybe this time.

The letter fluttered from her hand onto the table.

"Who was at the door?" Carson yelled from the top of the stairs.

Ebony looked down at the paper. Her whole body trembled as she leaned down sniffing the letter trying to pick up a scent, but nothing. She knew Leslie was crazy, but why would she be threatening her again? Hadn't she gotten over Carson by now? She wanted to run to her husband, but after the wedding episode, he already thought she was making a big deal out of nothing. She looked to the phone hanging on the wall needing to talk to someone but since Melody was on her honeymoon, she would have to wait. She studied the typed letter again looking for some sort of clue, but nothing.

"You didn't answer my question?" Carson came charging down the steps. Ebony grabbed the letter stuffing it in her robe.

"What?" She squinted her eyes at her husband who now wore his khakis and blue button up shirt ready for work.

"What is going on with you this morning?" Ebony sat motionless tuning out her husbands voice with her own thoughts in her head.

Carson stepped in between his wife's legs. He took his pointer finger running it down her chest into the opening of her robe.

"Maybe when I get home from work we can finish from this morning?" Her husbands hand slipped down cupping her breast.

"What is this?" He grabbed the piece of paper from her bosom opening it.

"Where did this come from? Who is it from?"

Ebony lowered her eyes at her husband. She knew all the wrong she played in their relationship last year, but Carson brought the crazy woman into their lives. He knew how much Leslie loved him and he should have left her alone. At least Jefferson wasn't crazy just a little damaged.

"You are asking me questions that obviously I can't answer."

His lips parted like he wanted to say something but he stopped. He grabbed his things and stormed out of the house. Ebony starred at the door amazed by the way her husband just reacted. Keeping things in, the way Carson always did. She could only image what his mind was thinking, probably that Jefferson was back in her life, but that was so far from the truth. She knew Leslie was behind this.

EIGHT

"I'm going out." Carson kissed his wife on the forehead as she sat at the kitchen table writing in a note pad.

"Where are you going?"

"Basketball." His wife dropped her pencil whipping around in her chair to look at him.

"Basketball? You haven't been since…"

"I know and it's time to go back. Be home later."

"You don't want me to go?"

"No I'm good."

Carson grabbed his gym bag and escaped out of the house as quickly as possible. He didn't want to tell his wife not to come, but the memories of her and Jefferson fill his brain. Basketball use to be his release until his wife changed all that by sleeping with someone else. The love Carson has for his wife is so strong that he put the infidelity behind him without ever thinking about it because he can't lose her.

"Nice to see you man." Michael shakes his boys hand along with the rest of the team who haven't seen him in months.

"I had to get out the house." Carson said lacing up his basketball shoes.

"Everything good at home?"

Yeah were fine."

Carson looked to the empty bleachers where his wife usually sat. He felt a sense of distance and loneliness from his wife that has been slowly forming since they got back from their honeymoon and when she starts going into the studio, things are going to get worse. How could he be sure that he could trust her with all the late nights and performances she will be doing? If she could cheat with someone he knew, what makes him think she wouldn't cheat with a complete stranger.

"You can play the first game." Mike motioned to the court. Carson made his way to the hard wood floor guarding his man. A tall figure about six feet moved into his space bumping him slightly. He turned to his left seeing an all too familiar face. Jefferson flashed a smile at him that turned him stomach. Even though he had claimed to forgive his wife for her indiscretion, he was not ready to face it again. I guess the rumor of him leaving town was just that.

"Good to see you man." Jefferson put one foot in front of Carson's guarding him in the front. Carson stepped back making space between them. He shot a look at his best friend warming the bench. Mike shrugged his shoulders not really comforting his friend. Two men over six feet were in the center of the court. The ball was tipped in Carson's direction. He grabbed it and took off dribbling down the court. Jefferson's bald head was caught in his peripheral. Jefferson stripped the ball from him just as he did his wife. Carson could feel the blood rush to his head. He sprinted after Jefferson now on the other side of the court. His opponent's feet lifted off the ground extending his long arms to the rim of the basket. Jefferson came down from his dunk meeting Carson's elbow on his jaw. All six feet of him went down.

"Oh Shit." Jefferson grabbed his mouth as blood started pouring from the open wound Carson had created. Jefferson jumped to his feet rushing towards Carson.

"Dirty B…" Jefferson leaped into Carson's arms tackling him to the ground. The two guys rolled around on the floor tussling. Jefferson's bloody right fist landed across Carson's cheek pressing it into the linoleum floor. Michael and two other men grabbed Jefferson pulling him off of Carson calming his flailing arms. Carson rose to his feet, grabbed his bag and left the gym.

"Carson wait." His best friend called after him but he kept walking angrily to his car. The dark sky fueled his anger for Jefferson. There so called peace that was established last year was obviously a facade. Carson's car was going fifteen miles over the speed limit. He reached his house in record time. His left cheek was throbbing and his hands shook as he turned the key taking it out of the ignition. His enemy's smug smile flashed through his mind and the thought of his wife grabbing his bald head and calling out his name infuriated him. Carson shook the steering wheel letting out a yell. Ebony opened the garage door starring into her husbands red eyes. He took a deep breath in not wanting to go into the house and face his wife. He watched her fold her arms and tap her foot. Carson opened the door slowly stepping out of the car.

"What are you doing?" her husband walked by without saying a word. "Mike called."

Ebony shut the door behind her husband. She made a small ice pack placing it on his cheek as he sat at the breakfast bar. Carson pulled back snatching the bag from her hands. She looked on wide eyed.

"Don't take your attitude out on me."

"I don't want to talk." Carson got up walking to the bedroom. He heard his wife's footsteps on the stairs behind him and knew that she would not let it go. He stepped into the bathroom turning on the shower. Catching a glimpse of his swollen cheek in the mirror fueled his anger even more for his wife and Jefferson. Anger that he should have dealt with last year, but now because he claimed to have forgiven her, he had to make good on that, but didn't know if that was possible. His one true love in life should have never had an affair with another man.

The hot water beat down his back as his head rested against the ceramic tiled shower. He closed his eyes enjoying the steam and the peace. A life that he use to have so much control over now seemed to be out of control. Jefferson had reappeared in his life to constantly remind him of his wife's dirty secret and now he couldn't even enjoy his weekly basketball games with his boys.

"Are you ready to tell me what happened?" His wife's quiet voice came from the other side of the shower curtain. Tears mixed with the water running down his face. Carson was thankful that the thin piece of plastic was blocking his view of his wife. His mouth opened letting water come in. He spit it back out before turning off the faucet. He dragged the shower curtain back exposing his wife sitting cross legged on the toilet.

"Ebony", he said quietly, "I really don't want to talk about it."

His wife looked blankly at him as he wrapped a towel around his waist. Carson stopped at the bathroom door turning to his wife.

"Just one question, have you seen Jefferson since last year?" Her head turned slowly as her eye brows turned in. Carson walked out of the bathroom already knowing his answer. His heart hurt to have to ask her that, but to calm his own conscious, it had to be said.

NINE

⌐⁓⌐

*E*bony woke up the next morning. The yellow and orange rays shone through the train window as she sat in the window seat riding into the city. Visions of her husband's hurt eyes kept flashing through her mind. She couldn't believe he thought she was seeing Jefferson again. What would make him think that? Ebony felt that she was trying to make their marriage work, but maybe not hard enough.

The train reached the city a little after 9 am. Ebony put four quarters in the homeless mans cup before climbing the dirty steps to the light on the city. She walked a few blocks from the subway station to the studio. Ebony stood on the stone pavement looking at the double doors starring at her reflection in the mirror tint of the glass. Her hands trembled as she reached for the door handle. Her future was just on the other side of the door. She dropped her hand, taking a step back from a dream that had existed since she was little. Was she really ready for this? After quitting both jobs, she would be putting everything she had into this dream and her new group of co workers. Jefferson crossed her mind at that moment. H had given her the courage to step foot on stage so many months ago. She needed that courage now to make her feet move through the double doors ahead. The door swung open being held be a young light skinned man with a clean shaven face walking out.

"Good morning." He said smiling at her. He stood there holding the door ajar. Ebony inhaled as her feet moved forward taking her into the building. She gave the young man a head nod and a half smile once inside. The door closed behind her sealing her fate. She blew out one long breath knowing this was her one shot. A smile came across her face and her feet tingled in her shoes. The long hallway that encompassed her was lined with framed gold records from great artists of her time, but many she had grown up listening to. Ebony ran her hands across several of them trying to feel the talent that they encompassed. She made her way down the hallway to a long, wooden receptionist desk. An older African American woman greeted her with a smile.

"Hello, my name is…"

"Mrs. Brody, I've been waiting for you."

"Hi Joe." Ebony turned her attention to Joe who came from around the corner wearing a huge grin which made her feel at ease.

"What's up love? You ready to lay down this track?" He kissed her forehead.

"I think so." Her voice trembled.

"You got this girl." Her eyes burned feeling droplets of water form in them. Someone she hardly knew had so much faith in her and she didn't want to let anyone down.

She reciprocated a smile to Joe before following him through several hallways to a sound proof hallway with two doors on each side. The couple walked into the room that had a number one above the door. It was a small studio with two cushioned office chairs in front of a huge sound board facing the enclosed booth with a single mike hanging from the ceiling and a standing microphone as well.

"I thought we would start with this song." Joe handed her a sheet of lyrics as he played a track for her.

"Ok, I like that. I've also been working on something of my own. She pulled out the lyrics that she wrote down the other night.

"Your eyes look sad and alone, and smile, no longer lights up the room…" Ebony sang the words for Joe. He closed his eyes moving his head to her words. Once she finished he opened his eyes with a blank look. Ebony held her breath not knowing what he thought of her first attempt at a song. His face lifted as he clasped his hands together.

"It's beautiful. I knew I was right about you. Now get your butt in that booth and let's do this."

Ebony threw her coat and purse into the first empty chair and scurried into the booth. She put the headphones on and the music started to play in her ears. Her lips parted and the sound flowed out. She sang the first song from her CD entitled Deceit. The image of that woman in black from the wedding flashed in her mind as well as the letter mysteriously dropped at her house that morning. Her voice trembled and the music went out in her ears.

"Cut." Joe called. Ebony pulled her headphones off knowing she had failed. She knew it would take several tries to get the track right, but in her heart she knew she couldn't sing with so much on her mind. Joe waved to her to come out.

"What's going on sweetheart?"

"I think Jefferson's sister is still after me?"

"That's the price of fame baby." He chuckled then stopped once he saw the sternness in her face.

She rolled her eyes. "I'm serious. I thought I saw her the other day and I got a letter at my house and I'm not famous."

"Well you will be and you can't let other people determine your future." Ebony smiled at him softly brushing her anxiety aside. "Now get your butt in that booth before I charge you for this session."

She stepped into the sound booth, rolled her neck and shoulders around then grabbed the headphones. Her sweating palms grabbed the standing microphone. She closed her eyes as the music hit her ears again. Her lips parted and the song belted from her diaphragm. Five hours later the track was done along with the song she had written.

"That was great." Ebony flopped into the chair next to Joe as he finished up the track. He played it from start to finish. It felt like an out of body experience as Ebony heard her voice. She thought of her father thinking how proud he would be at this moment and how she wanted to share this with him. Carson didn't seem as interested in her music career as she had hoped and her mother was still grieving. Ebony felt there was no one to share her excitement with except Joe.

"We have seven more tracks so we do have a long week ahead of us and the company is planning a huge album release party. Lots of people believe in you."

"This is all so unreal to me." Her feet danced on the floor.

"What else you got for me?" She asked hyped up.

Joe turned to his standing keyboard in the corner and started planning.

"I created this the other day." He started playing a tune and words started coming out of her mouth. She had no idea where they came from but she sang from the heart about her new passions.

"We should put this down." Ebony looked down at her watch noticing that it was past 6pm and her husband would be expecting his dinner in thirty minutes. She looked to Joe and the excitement on his face and back down at her watch. Against her better judgment she texted her husband saying that she would not be home for a few hours. She could hear the disappointment in his text back to her, but this was work and it comes first.

"I'm going to order a pizza. I think we will be here for a little longer."

Ebony stepped back into the booth as Joe ordered the food. She definitely had some making up to do although after the rejection in the shower this morning, her husband could make it up to her too.

TEN

"My wife left me alone, you wanna grab some dinner?" Carson asked Michael as they walked into the locker room at the gym.

"Your wife is coming home late and all you want to do is go out to dinner? I can think of something better to do."

"We do have to eat." Carson snapped the white towel at his boy that was wrapped around his neck and you know I'm not like that.

"We need to eat, but not food. Did you see that woman in the pink tight pants out there? Good God what I would love to do to her."

"I'm glad some things don't change." Carson grabbed his gym bag and headed for the showers. The first day of Ebony's new life and she was already staying out late. She knows how he likes his schedule, especially during the week and this was not acceptable but then again his whole life felt like it was changing for the worse.

Carson stood in the mirror brushing his hair after slipping on his khakis, a black polo shirt and a pair of brown loafers.

"You need a makeover." Mike walked up behind him in a baggy pair of jeans, a loose white button up shirt, and some dark tan dress shoes.

Carson looked down at his clothes. "What's wrong with me?"

"Your whole closet is polo shirts and khakis, boring."

"I'm not you, trying to catch a different woman every night. My wife likes me like this, that's all that matters."

"Are you sure about that?" Carson squinted at his sarcastic friend. He shook off his comment, grabbed his gym bag, and followed his friend out the gym.

Michael whipped his white Lexus into a dimly lit parking lot with a pink neon sign that flashed a naked girl on the roof.

"Man I am not up for this."

"Relax a little. Let's go."

The guys walked into the small bar. There was about two dozen guys ranging from old to young surrounded the bar.

"What's up Rock?" Michael gave a hand shake to the huge bald headed bouncer at the door. "Your table is open."

Carson turned to his friend, eyes wide.

"You come here a lot?"

"Not everyone is wholesome like you." Michael's mysterious grin led them to a small curved booth in the dimly lit part of the club.

"Why do you sit back here?"

"If you sit up front then the girls expect you to tip and not all these females get my money. You gotta earn it."

A thin young girl trying to walk in very high heels with her painted toes hanging over the edge of them walked up to the guys.

"Two beers and two shots of absolute please." She shuffled off in the direction of the bar. Carson slumped into the booth wanting to be anywhere but there. He pulled out his cell phone hoping to see a text from his wife, but nothing. What was she doing in the studio so late and how many men was she around? She had cheated before. Had she lost sight of their marriage again and betrayed him? The skinny girl approached with the drinks. Carson grabbed a shot glass from her tray taking it back.

"Another one please?" He slammed the glass on the table.

"That's what I'm talking about."

"I got demons in my head. My wife is the love of my life, but I think about her and Jefferson constantly. His dirty hands on her and his you know all inside of what's mine."

Michael drank from the beer bottle eyes wide.

"That will make you crazy man." Michael put his hand in the air waxing towards someone. Several minutes later a few half naked dancers joined the men in their corner.

"Just enjoy tonight."

Carson relaxed into the cushion allowing a young caramel colored girl spread his legs open, straddle him and give him a lap dance. The girl tossed her long, black weave around whipping Carson in the face.

"Touch it," She demanded of Carson as she rounded her butt in his face. His hand rounded the bottom curve of her bare butt. The stripper flashed her white teeth at him before moving on to her next patron. Carson brought his hand to his nose smelling the sweet oil he wiped off of her.

"I'm going to wash my hand. I can't go home smelling like a stripper."

Carson stood up as his best friend laughed at him while stuffing several ones down a young, perky pair of breasts. He made his way through the crowd of horny men and working women.

"Men, turn towards center stage and give it up for Carmen." The DJ announced.

Carson stopped turning towards center stage. A very slender girl with a natural bush strutted on the stage placing two hands on the medal pole and swinging in a circle before wrapping her legs around it and sliding to the bottom into a split. Carson leaned his head in closer recognizing the female.

"Oh my gosh." He quickly ducked into the bathroom splashing cold water on his face as soon as he reached the sink. Why was his sister in law twirling on a pole half naked? Was he supposed to question her or better yet, does he tell his wife that her sister is a stripper? Too many questions were running through his head. The only fact he knew for sure was that he could not go out there and watch her get naked in front of him. That would be a true violation and he would never be able to look her in the eye at another family function again.

Carson scurried out of the bathroom trying to stay out of the eye sight of India.

"Man we gotta go." Michael looked up with a grin on his face until he saw the seriousness of his best friend. Carson motioned his head slightly to the stage. Michael followed then immediately jumped up leading the way to the door.

"Damn she put me in a bad spot." Carson spoke as soon as they were outside the club.

"Are you going to tell your wife?" Michael sniggled as they climbed into his car.

"I don't know. I don't think it's my place, but I can't keep a secret from her."

"Not all secrets are bad." Michael sped off down the road as Carson starred out the window into the night wondering what he was supposed to do. After all India is grown and could make her own decisions.

ELEVEN

"Morning." Ebony rolled on her right side facing her husband. Her eyes blinked trying to focus on her husbands face. She looked past his ear noticing the digital clock on the nightstand. Nine fifteen on a Sunday was late for Carson. She ran her hand down his cheek looking into his exhausted eyes.

"How was your night?"

"I went out with Mike. I should have stayed home."

She smiled slightly.

"You look like something else is bothering you." Carson twisted his body to face the ceiling. His wife propped herself up to look directly into his eyes.

"I'm fine."

She mocked her husband who rolled his eyes at her before rolling off the side of the bed walking into the bathroom.

Ebony lay back down against her pillow still on a high from her recording session. Joe wanted to take her to Atlanta to play a few gigs at some local clubs. She knew Carson would hate the idea so she had to find a way to break it to him. She knew her husband was holding something in and secrets were not her thing anymore. Ebony followed her husband into the bathroom. She put the toilet seat down and took a seat. Carson flicked the switch to his razor making slow strokes across his face then combing his facial hair to repeat the same process. Their eyes met in the square mirror hanging on the wall.

"What?" Carson snapped.

"You're withholding information and you're a bad liar."

"I'm just saying, check on your sister and me from time to time, or do what you want to."

He put the razor down in the sink before storming out of the bathroom.

"My sister, you?" The rhythmic pounding in her chest began to pick up as she followed her husband out of the bathroom. The bedroom was empty. She stammered down the steps the find Carson in the kitchen reading the news paper.

Ebony poured herself a cup of coffee. She had started drinking more since she quit her job. She picked up her cell phone texting her sister. No response.

Ebony jumped up on the breakfast bar positioning her body in front of her husband. She parted her legs letting her pink teddy slide up her thighs.

"Well my night was great Joe and I got into a groove and it was incredible. He is so funny, driven, and just plain talented. I think we will work well together."

"Damn, did you fuck him too?" Ebony's eyes grew big. Her husband pushed her aside standing up. She snapped her legs together hugging herself feeling dirty.

Carson rubbed his head pacing. "I'm sorry. That came out wrong."

"No." She put her finger up. "You are just speaking truth. You haven't gotten over what happened with Jefferson. I knew it." Her husband turned back to her placing his hand on her knee. She pulled back crossing her legs.

"So now what?"

His fist pounded the breakfast bar.

"Why did you break us? I can deal with lots, but that broke me and to see him again…"

Ebony hopped off the counter.

"You sure acted cool last year. Why now. Is that why you've been so distant to me? You won't touch me or make love to me since the Poconos."

Ebony caressed her husband's back as he leaned over the breakfast bar.

"I wish you would have said something to me earlier."

Her husband stood up to face her.

"What do we do now?"

"Maybe I need to talk to someone."

"Yes me." Her hands reached out to touch her husband's who were bawled up. His tear stricken eyes met hers. Carson took one step back so her hands wouldn't touch his. Her mouth opened. Ebony backed away from her husband. The realization of his pain just hit her. Carson was quiet and kept things inside but his hurt was all over his face. Ebony sat back watching her husband pace around the kitchen. He stopped kicking the wooden kitchen chair over. Sweat droplets covered his forehead.

"I love you... I love us. But now it's all about your career and I don't know if I can be second."

Her husband stormed out rattling the windows as he slammed the door. Ebony ran to the front door looking out the small window that circled the door. She watched her husband's car speed off down the street. What had gotten into him? She had never seen him act that way. There must be something else going on, if only he would talk to her. Ebony poured herself a cup of black coffee watching the little bubbles dance around the cup until they disappeared. Carson's last words rang over in her mind. It seemed like he didn't want her to succeed. For the first time in a long time she was excited about her future and making a career for herself that she could be proud of and she thought she had the full support of her husband, but maybe not.

Her cell phone danced around the kitchen counter.

"Hello."

"I only got married, I didn't flee the country. You can still call a bitch once in a while."

Ebony's face lit up. "Melody, I have missed you. Sorry I have been so preoccupied. How are you?"

"We aren't talking about me. I called to check on you."

"I could really use my best friend. Are you free to do lunch?"

The phone grew silent. "Sure." Ebony hung up running up stairs.

....

The afternoon sun beat down on the small outside patio area of a little Italian restaurant in the heart of Little Italy.

"Hey Chica." Melody approached the two -seater wire table in a long blonde wig, big golden sunglasses and a yellow mini sundress. Ebony stood hugging her best friend.

"I have missed you. I see you started without me."

Melody pointed to the glass of white wine that was on the table.

"I need this right now." Melody tilted her head to the right.

"What's wrong?" Melody grabbed the glass of water the older waiter had placed on the black wire table.

"It's Carson. He got into a fight with Jefferson and he thinks I'm cheating on him again. We fought and I don't know what to do. I've never seen him like this before."

Melody's mouth fell open. "You're kidding?"

"No. He stormed out the house and I don't know if he's coming back."

That man loves you. He's not going any where." Ebony took a long sip from her wine glass hoping her best friend was right. She ordered a big plate of spaghetti while her bestie ordered chicken parmesan.

"So how's married life?" Ebony was waiting for a huge grin to pass on her best friends face but it didn't.

"It's good. The honeymoon is definitely over though."

The server left two small green salads in front of the ladies. Ebony lifted her fork starring at her friend. She had never seen her eat with sunglasses on. She cocked her head from left to right knowing there was definitely something wrong. Melody put a fork full of lettuce in her mouth chewing slowly.

"Well I have news. I'm going to a few cities to perform in some clubs and it comes at the best time because Carson and I could use some distance, I just haven't told him yet."

Melody gave her best friend a half smile as she took her napkin dabbing under her glasses.

"Where is my best friend?" Her best friend's head dropped down. She slowly pulled her golden glasses from her face exposing a colorful collage of greens, reds, and purples around her right eye.

"What the hell". Ebony's fork clinked against the glass plate as she starred at her best friend.

"You should see his face." Her best friend laughed uneasy.

Ebony scooted her chair closer to her friend. "Don't you dare do that. I will kick his ass."

"He thought I was cheating and from my past, I can't blame him."

Ebony leaned back in her chair biting her bottom lip. The waiter dropped their food down in front of them. Ebony disregarded her noisy stomach, pushing her plate to the side.

She made her fist towards her best friend leaning forward. Melody never moved.

"What am I to do? I am not going to sit here and let this happen."

"You're making a big deal of nothing. How long have you known me? I'm not letting any man put his hands on me."

"You want to come to Atlanta with me? I have three performances."

Ebony slides her plate in front of her picking up her fork.

"I think it's just bad timing."

"I need a chaperone."

Melody and Ebony's eyes met. The two starred intensely at each other.

TWELVE

———— ⚍ ————

*C*aron's car pulled up in the driveway late that evening. He hated fighting with his wife and felt stupid for starting a fight over nothing. He had forgiven her last year after the Jefferson/Leslie fiasco and now he was going back on his word and letting it bother him. That was his issue, not hers. He turned his car off wanting to tell his wife that he was sorry and should not have questioned her loyalty at this point in their relationship. If he could, he would have stayed in their honeymoon bliss forever but they came back to reality and everything changed.

His wife's car was not in the garage. She hadn't texted him saying that she was not going to be home. Upon entering the house, he saw a white piece of paper taped to the refrigerator. He grabbed the note from his wife. He grabbed the edge of the bar stool steadying himself to take a seat. She had left for a few days without saying so much as a word, just a note. The paper slipped from his grasp falling onto the breakfast bar. How could she leave without saying a word? His first thought was to surprise her on her trip, but she hadn't even said where she went so maybe she didn't want to be disturbed. Carson pulled his cell phone from his back pocket bringing his wife's name up. He started to text her then put the phone back down. He decided to honor her privacy and leave her alone, but when she came back, he definitely wanted to make amends and fix their relationship before it got out of hand.

....

The ladies plane touched down in Atlanta shortly after six pm. Melody leaped up from her seat as soon as the seat belt sign light went off. She was already in first class so it wasn't like they had to make a mad dash to the front of the plane. Ebony giggled at her friend's excitement. She knew that bringing her on this trip was the best thing for her right now. Carson would forgive her eventually but she had to put space between her best friend and her abusive husband.

A nice looking slender light skinned man stood inside the airport terminal holding a sign with her name on it.

"That has never happened before."

Melody turned to her best friend, face tense. "If I haven't told you, I am really proud of you." Ebony's eye browns lifted as she gave her best friend a hug. Her eyes burned but she refused to cry. The two shared a quick hug then turned back to the man in front of them.

"I'm James. It's nice to meet you. I'm going to take you to the hotel and whatever you need all weekend, I'm here for you honey." James took the ladies carry on bags as they walked down to baggage claim.

"Girl, I love this bag. I need to go to New York. You all get all the good stuff."

Melody glanced at Ebony giggling at James flamboyant ways.

"We are going to have a great weekend."

"James, where is there good food to eat. A bitch is hungry." Melody cried out as they climbed in the back of the black sedan.

"You in Atlanta baby, everything is good including the men, okay."

James handed the ladies two champagne flutes. The best friends clinked their glasses together before taking a sip. Ebony relaxed into the leather seats as they watched the city lights through the tinted windows.

James dropped the ladies off at the Marriot downtown.

"I'll see you girls in the morning. Get some sleep or not." He winked at them before pulling off. The ladies dropped their luggage off in their suite on the fifteenth floor.

"I gotta eat."

"Okay greedy. Let's get something to eat downstairs."

The dimly lit hotel restaurant was half full. Large red drapes covered the tall walls. The two sat at a two top table in the back corner of the restaurant.

"What are you having?" Ebony asked browsing the menu.

"I want some dick." Ebony couched, chocking on the water that the young server had set before her.

"You are still a married woman." Melody cocked her head to the side giving her friend a dirty look.

"Ok I know, I know." Her best friend had made her feel the shame of her affair all over again. The pain, regret, pleasure, sorrow, and pure enjoyment of the year rushed through her brain. She grinned as her eyes fought off tears at the same time. She still hated herself for what she had done to her husband but after spending half of her life with someone, it's hard to fight off the advances of someone who makes you feel sexy and alive even if it were just a trick.

"Ebony?" Melody snapped her fingers in front of her friend. "What are you eating?"

"Oh sorry, I'll have seafood Alfredo." She handed her menu to the server.

"What's going on in that head of yours?"

"Just preoccupied with my shows I guess."

"Are you nervous?"

Being in a strange city was somewhat calming for her. No familiar faces in the audience but also the thought of people not supporting her feared her.

"No, I'm good." Ebony's eye twitched as she took a sip from her wine glass.

"We need to go to that famous strip club while were here."

"We need to talk about your husband and your situation." Melody shifted in her chair. Ebony reached across the table to grab her best friend's hands.

"You are the strongest person I know, but this, you should not put up with."

"If I try to divorce him, it may get worse. I don't know how crazy he is." Her best friend's eyes were scared for the first time. Not like the fear on her wedding day, but truly scared for her life. Melody squeezes her best friend's hands as her forehead hits the table. This was a first. Ebony has never seen her friend like this. She opened her mouth to speak then closed it. Her head tilted to the side then down. Her mouth opened again then closed. Ebony rubbed the back of her best friend's weave lightly so not to mess it up. Their server approached the table holding a large round tray with two dishes on it. Ebony squeezed Melody's hand and she sat up from the table. Ebony looked up as the server sat her pasta dish in front of her. She spotted a bald headed man with broad shoulders and a great sense of style. Ebony crossed her legs feeling warmth between them. She poked her noodles with her fork before twirling it in them. She brought the fork to her lips filling her mouth. She watched the stranger shift in his bar stool, sip from his small glass of dark liquor, mesmerized by his sexiness. The stranger swiveled slightly on the bar stool.

"Oh my gosh." Ebony slunk down in her seat trying to hide under the table.

"What are you doing?" Melody turned in her seat noticing the stranger.

"Oh wow." She quickly turned back around hoping not to be noticed.

"Hello ladies." Ebony peeked up over the table.

"Hello". The two women exhaled together and shared a laugh. The man could have been Jefferson's twin.

"I was sitting at the bar and just wanted to let you know how stunning you are."

Ebony's cheeks turned rosy.

"Thank you." Ebony replied.

"You should come see her perform tomorrow night at Casper's."

"Only if I can buy her a drink afterwards."

"Will do." Ebony felt like a child at the grown ups table as Melody basically tried to set her up with a stranger. Just because her marriage was questionable did not mean Ebony was going to step out on her husband again. That was one mistake she wished she could erase from her memory; at least some of it.

"I think I'm done eating." Ebony flagged down the waitress to get the check.

"Now what are we to do with the rest of the night?" Melody grinned.

"I want to find something to get into." Melody winked at a tall, dark and handsome man at the bar.

"Ok, I guess I'll see you later."

Her best friend joined the man at the bar as she wandered out of the restaurant not ready to retrieve to the hotel room for the rest of the night.

Ebony walked out of the hotel to the street. With no destination in sight, she walked up and down the streets seeing the up coming holiday take form with ghosts and fake witches appearing in windows of the shops. She watched couples walk hand and hand questioning her decision to bring her best friend instead of her husband. She thought about Carson eating carry out all alone in front of the television while he watched the news. She dug in her purse for her cell phone but couldn't dial the number. She had nothing to say that could be done over the phone. Their relationship had become so distant that she didn't even have words for her own husband.

After what seemed like an hour, Ebony decided to return to her hotel room. She swiped the key card when she reached the room. She opened the door to pure darkness.

"Melody?" She heard female moans coming from the back. Her hand rubbed the wall until she hit the light switch bringing light to her best friend's bare butt in the air as she rode Mr. Tall, dark, and handsome from the bar.

"Oh my gosh. I'm so sorry." Ebony apologized.

"It's ok, if you want to join us." The stranger flashed a huge smile.

"She's not like that." Melody answered for her best friend who could barely close her mouth. Ebony backed out of the room slamming the door behind her. She looked up and down the empty hallway before slinking to the floor. She pulled out her phone to check her email while she waited. Knowing her best friend, she may be waiting for a while. Ebony kicked her shoes off crossing her legs. Carson had still not reached out to her. This was not a good sign. He was probably pissed that she had left with just a note.

THIRTEEN

*C*arson sat in front of the television watching the nightly news as he ate his take out from the Chinese restaurant on the corner by his job.

"This is so sad." He picked up the remote flipping through the channels. He twirled his fork in his shrimp fried rice having lost his appetite. He looked to his phone realizing he wasn't even a second thought for his wife. Would this be their life now where she is off touring and he would be left home alone? He has always wanted his wife to succeed but why should he have to suffer. The two of them had to have a serious conversation about the future of their relationship when she returned home.

Carson pushed his food aside and text his boy to see what he was up to. Like his wife, he got no response. He changed out of his khakis and polo shirt and threw on some jeans and a New York Giants t-shirt and a baseball hat. He ended up at the strip club where he had become a regular since his wife had abandoned him. Carson walked in heading straight for the bar.

"Hey sugar, nice to see you again. Beer please?"

Carson gave her a half smile and a head nod. He never thought he would be a regular in a place like this, but he was only here for one reason, well maybe two. The main bar stage had a beautiful Brazillian woman with long black hair and a lime green thong lying on the stage with her legs extended in the air. Carson turned his head as she spread her legs open feeling guilty. He turned to the smaller stage and noticed India who was wearing a curly blonde wig and a black lace teddy as she twirled around the pole. There was no safe place for his eyes so he focused on the bottles disappearing from the top of his beer. Carson was never a loud man, but he thought of himself as a protector and provider. He turned back to his sister in law who had an obviously drunk man gazing at her from the bottom of the stage. The older Caucasian man took his hand and rubbed it over her chest. India backed away out of his arm reach. Carson stood up. India climbed to the top of the pole hugging it tightly with her thighs, hanging upside down. Her thighs released slowly as she inched down to the ground. An uproar of applause echoed through the small club. Carson's lips parted. He had seen this girl become a woman. He had known her since she was four and now to see her doing this was more than he could take. India walked off the stage, fixing her clothes as she approached her brother in law.

"Hey bro, you have been here a lot. I think my perfect sister isn't doing her job in the bedroom." India fell back into his arms. His nose hairs burned from her breath as he caught her.

"Are you drunk?"

"Are you?" India stood upright stammering a little.

"I gotta get you out of here."

"I need to please my clients." She waved at a young man sitting in the VIP section pointing at his crotch.

"No really, you are done."

Carson took her hand and dragged her out of the club.

They pulled up at the Brody household. Carson turned to India who had fallen asleep. If Ebony could see this situation right now, she would be pissed. He smirked. Carson picked her body up from the passenger side carrying her into the house, laying her on the couch and covering her with a throw.

"You are too good for her." Carson jerked covering his heart with his hand.

"I thought you were sleep."

She turned to face him and his eyes dropped as her left breast peeked from the side of her teddy. Carson stepped back needing space between them. He had never looked at another woman except for his brief period with Leslie, but this was wrong, this was his wife's sister.

"I need a drink." Carson walked off to a small wooden cupboard pulling out a small brown bottle. India walked up behind him with the throw around her shoulders.

"Pour me one."

"I think you've had enough." India snatched the small glass that he had poured for himself.

"I am grown." She chugged the drink extending her hand for a refill. India returned to the couch when her glass was full. Carson followed.

He took a small sip from his glass. "Could you put something on? You know where your sister's stuff is."

India smirked putting her head down. "Does this make you uncomfortable?" India stands up showing off her skimpy outfit. Carson looked her up and down noticing her perky nipples that seemed to be starring right at him. He crossed his legs feeling his manhood get excited.

"Stop playing girl." Carson tilts in his favorite chair. "Really India, why are you doing this? What is going on?"

India's bottom lip trembled as she brought the glass of rum to her lips. Her pupils moved from right to left very slowly. There was no happiness in her face and Carson knew that she was not stripping because she wanted to. There was something deeper going on with her. Carson got up and took a seat on the floor in front of the couch.

"We are family and I want you to be able to confide in me. What is going on with you? I know your not dancing because you like it, that's not you." India crossed her beautiful brown skinned legs in front of him. Her black painted toe nails dangled in front of his nose smelling of a mixture of peach and strawberries. She slid her body down to the carpet with him.

"I lost my father too not just Ebony. I know they were close, but she's not the only one feeling pain and I've been at that house helping my mother get by everyday, not her." India took the glass from Carson empting it. "Sometimes I hate her and her perfect little life." She said quietly. He put his arm around her as she fell into his body fitting right into his underarm. He pulled the blonde wig off seeing how vulnerable she was. He rubbed her natural hair thinking back to the time India threatened a 300 pound line backer in high school for messing with her sister. She was fearless, but the woman he was holding was not that same woman.

All the weight of her head fell on him. Carson grabbed the blanket from the couch, covering them. He leaned his head on top of India's closing his eyes as well.

....

The rays of sun and the smell of bacon woke Carson. He leaned up from the carpet feeling the effects of having slept on the floor all night. Peeking over the couch he saw India dancing around the kitchen as she cooked breakfast. She had on one of his NYU t-shirts that came down to her knees and nothing else. The sunlight from the kitchen window shadowed half her face making her look beautiful. Carson thought back to her twenty-first birthday party. Her parents had thrown her a surprise party at the house. She had walked through the door with a girl friend in a short mini skirt and boots that came to her knees. She was a little tipsy and was glowing. That was the first time Carson had seen her as a young woman and not Ebony's little sister. Mike had asked his best friend to hook him up with India that night, but Carson wouldn't have it.

"You're awake."

"What? Oh yes, morning. It smells great in here." Carson rose to his feet.

"Come on sleepy head, let's eat." India placed two plates of pancakes, bacon and eggs on the breakfast bar.

"Thank you for this." Carson said as he sat on the stool. "Your sister doesn't cook for me anymore so this is great." He cut through the stack of pancakes with his fork filling his mouth.

"Well how about dinner?" Carson coughed and took a big gulp of orange juice. His wife did leave him alone and he missed the company.

"Why not?" India smiled as they ate their breakfast in silence.

FOURTEEN

"*G*irl get up." Melody nudged her friend. Ebony opened her eyes seeing her best friend standing over her with her wig to the side and a silk robe wrapped around her.

"Could you back up? I can see up your robe and I don't want to see that." Ebony sat up rubbing her tired eyes.

"I'm sure she is smiling at you right now." Melody was grinning from ear to ear.

"Really bitch? You're nasty." Ebony stood up stretching her back. "I have a show tonight. Next time remind me to get two rooms."

"How about I buy you breakfast?" Her best friend fluttered her eyes.

"That's the least you can do."

Ebony jumped in the shower washing off the dirt from the grungy hotel carpet that served as her bed the night before. She laughed to herself remembering all the nights at college when she used to sleep on the couch in their dorm lobby because Melody had a man in the room. She should have known that this would happen although she thought the marriage would have changed her and they still haven't talked about the black eye that had just cleared up from her face.

Thirty minutes later, Ebony joined her best friend who was sipping on coffee in the hotel restaurant. She looked like she was pondering something very heavy.

"What is wrong?" Ebony pulled out the rose padded chair. She motioned for the older lady who was the server to ask for some orange juice.

"I just got off the phone with my lovely husband who ordered me to come home."

Ebony reached out grabbing her best friend's shaky hand.

"What is really going on? I don't think you're telling me everything." Melody's chest heaved as she lets out a long breath.

"He just has a temper at times. I think because of my past he just doesn't trust me."

She brought the coffee mug to her lips but didn't sip.

"That doesn't give him the right to put his hands on you."

"But what am I supposed to do?" She puts her cup down. "I can't leave him, he will come for me. I knew I shouldn't have gotten married. That dick had me hooked. I knew it was too good to be true."

Ebony slammed her open hands on the table leaning into her friend. "Why are you making jokes?"

"I'm not. His dick did have me hooked so when he asked me to marry him, I couldn't say no."

"Even though you're not the marrying type?"

She shook her head slowly in agreement.

Ebony leaned back in her chair glaring at her best friend of more than twenty years. Melody was the strong, funny, and confident one. All the traits that Ebony wished she possessed. Melody was always her rock but now she needed to be hers. Water filled Ebony's eyes as she starred at her friend. No words came to her lips.

The server brought a stack of three pancakes with a scoop of butter and syrup dripping down the sides and sat it in front of Ebony. She placed a cheese omelet with a few slices of oranges decorating the plate in front of Melody.

"I don't like this at all." Ebony shook her fork before stabbing her pancakes with it. Her appetite had left her but she knew she needed to keep her strength up for later.

"I want to fix this." Melody placed her hand over her best friends. That was her way of saying that everything would be ok and for Ebony not to worry about her. Ebony hated when she did that to her but she knew her best friend had such a strong personality that she was going to do whatever she wanted to and no one could stop her.

The ladies ate their breakfast making small talk but not speaking of their husbands or their relationships again. Carson always made Ebony pancakes when she was sad or had something weighing on her. This was her first real performance away from home. Her husband wasn't here and the one person who she wanted to call to calm her nerves was no longer on Earth. The whole situation felt wrong.

....

Ebony's palms were drenched as she pulled up at the ritzy night club that was rented out just for her tonight. It seemed like a fairy tale come true pulling up in a stretch limo that the record company had sent for her. The thought of driving her Honda Accord to an event like this was unimaginable. That would be the first upgrade when her first real money started coming in. She checked her compact mirror for lipstick on her teeth. All good. The driver opened the door allowing her four inch black stilettos to touch the red carpet laid out. Ebony straightened her black dress as she stood making sure the triangle cut outs were on her sides like they were meant to be. Lights flashed, blinding her vision as she made her way to the front door being held open by two big, bald headed Caucasian men. Anger for her husband appeared. She did not want to walk in alone and if Carson really loved her he would have found a way to be with her tonight and skip work.

The club was dimly lit filled with the sounds of trumpets, horns, and a light steady drum beat as people of all colors walked around in their Sunday best. To the right was an all white VIP area, a square bar in the center of the room and a small dance floor to the back of the club. Ebony looked around for her best friend. Melody came charging towards her with a huge grin plastered on her face and the man from last night following behind her like a puppy.

"Aaahhh. This is nice girl. We have arrived." Ebony giggled at her crazy friend and her tiny red skirt which is why every man's eyes were focused on her protruding back side and an off the shoulder black top.

"You look great."

"This is Darren." She introduced the stranger from the night before.

"Let's get a drink." She grabbed her best friend's hand leading her to the bar. Ebony spotted Joe in the VIP area putting her index finger up towards him. Melody ordered two martinis from the young female bartender then they went to the white area sitting in the comfy arm chairs.

"Hi Joe." He leaned down kissing his new prodigy on the cheek.

"You ready for your coming out party?"

Ebony grinned showing her teeth. "I am, but I'm very nervous."

"Drink up you'll do great." Melody said pointing to her glass.

"I'm sorry your husband couldn't be here."

Ebony gave a half smile knowing he could have taken the short plane ride to surprise her and support her. But maybe this was his way of saying he really didn't support her career and that would cause her to make some really hard life decisions.

"I'm all she needs." Melody gave her best friend a light squeeze.

Ebony giggled uneasily as she relaxed into her chair. She scanned the club looking at all the people wondering who they were because she didn't know any of them and was sure she did not have a fan base yet. Ebony watched the entrance way as she sipped on her drink. A tall but familiar man entered the room. The dim light shone off his bald head like the Mr. Clean man. His brown blazer hung off his shoulder, the off white shirt had the two top buttons open and a pair of baggy blue jeans fit his waist perfectly. Their eyes connected and Ebony's heart slowed. The music seemed to fade out as no one else existed at that moment. A tingle started in the tips of her fingers and ran all the way to her toes. There he was the man who helped get her to this place, the man that use to pleasure her body and the man she had started to have feeling for almost a year ago. Jefferson was less than thirty feet from her. Her feet didn't know weather to run towards the door or into his arms. She wanted to ask him if he sent that note to her house the other day to scare her and why. Jefferson gave her a half smile.

"Ebony?" Melody nudged her best friends shoulder.

"What?"

"Are you listening? What are you starring at?"

She motioned her head towards the door.

"I thought I saw someone I knew."

Ebony whipped her head back towards the door. Jefferson was gone. Ebony stood up looking around the club. He had disappeared into thin air.

"Let's go superstar. You're up." Joe extended his hand helping Ebony out of her seat.

"Wish me luck." She turned to her best friend and her new friend with a nervous smile. Joe led her to the back to a small dressing room.

"You got about twenty minutes to get ready."

Joe disappeared into the darkness of the club shutting the door behind him. A beautiful emerald dress was draped on the back of a chair that sat in front of a vanity. She put her purse on the vanity taking out her small makeup bag.

"Delivery." She jumped dropping her lipstick tube to the floor. Ebony's wet hand grabbed the door handle pulling it open.

"Thank you." She said grabbing the vase of a dozen red roses and placing it on the vanity. Her face lit up. She knew Carson would not let her down. If he couldn't be here physically, he would be here mentally. She dug in the flowers lifting the small white card from them reading the message.

"Don't break a leg or anything else."

A tingle ran through her body. She peeked her head out the doorway, but the delivery man was no where in sight. Quickly closing the door, she locked it. Who sent the letter to her house and now these flowers? It had to be Jefferson messing with her mind. What could he possibly want with her now? He had come between her marriage with his mind-blowing sex and allowed his crazy sister to harm her. It was no coincidence that she had seen him here tonight.

"Ten minutes." Joe yelled from the other side of the door. Ebony threw the card down not being able to put any more focus towards this nonsense right now. She grabbed the green dress changing quickly. She checked her hair and make up one more time before heading to the stage. Joe introduced her and she took the stage. The spot light was blinding which gave her a strange feeling of comfort not being able to see the faces starring back at her. Her very first performance with Jefferson crossed her mind. The way he calmed her nerves which is what she needed right now.

A young guy who was the host of the show gave her a small introduction. Her music came on over the sound system. Ebony starred out at the blank faces of the audience. Her chest rose holding in a deep breath. She let out a long breath of air as the sounds came out of her mouth. Her eyes focused on the spot lights in the back of the club as she sang her heart out in the quiet club. She sang two more songs before the audience decided that they liked her with a loud applause.

Walking back down the hallway after her fifteen minute set, the roar from the crowd echoed the hallways. Ebony skipped to her dressing room feeling a thrill like no other.

"Great feeling huh?" Joe asked as he appeared behind her catching her before she opened the door.

"The thrill, the nerves… it was great."

Ebony pushed open the door to the dressing room. Water ran to the tip of her toes as the floor was covered with her broken vase of roses. Her hands covered her open mouth as she took a step back into the hallway. Joe's arm crossed her chest pushing her aside. He scanned the room looking for anyone or anything suspicious.

"All clear." Ebony had stepped behind him beginning to pick up pieces of petals from the floor. She brought the petal to her nose smelling the sweetness. The small card looked like confetti amongst the petals.

"I'm good Joe." She said quietly. She escorted him out closing the door behind him. She sat on the small tan couch in the corner. She brought her knees into her chest like the night of her father's funeral. Less than an hour ago she was so happy and now her strange reality was back. Was someone messing with her or wanted to hurt her? It didn't make sense unless Jefferson's crazy sister was out of the nut house or he wanted to hurt her for some unsettling reason.

"Hi." Two simple letters formed a word that pierced her ears. Ebony froze, afraid to look up and face the owner of the voice but she knew it all too well that she didn't have to look. She looked down spotting the shiny gold tipped shoes.

"You're not speaking to me?" The blood in her body went from her head to her feet causing them to burn slightly. Her mind was telling her to run out of the room to safety but the rest of her couldn't move. The shoes slid closer to her.

"I knew you were meant to be a star. You are still as gorgeous as I remember."

He took a few more steps to her. She arched her head up looking into his dreamy brown eyes. His manly hands tucked a small piece of loose hair behind her ear letting his middle finger linger on her ear lobe. Her bottom half throbbed responding to his touch.

"I've missed this beautiful body and those lips." His finger stopped right on her bottom lip pulling on it gently.

"Is this you're doing?" She yanked her head back out of his touch. "Are you stalking me?"

He chuckled in that overly confident way of his.

"First, don't flatter yourself. You are incredible, but so am I. Stalking is not my forte, but it looks like someone is messing with you." He lifted his feet up looking at the water dripping from the bottom of his expensive shoes.

She starred at him trying to see past his arrogance. Jefferson walked back to the door shutting it, turning the silver lock counter clockwise. Ebony took a deep breath.

"I miss you." He blurted out

Ebony rolled her eyes. "You tried to ruin me."

"I didn't know the truth. I was all about revenge. I never imagined my own sister was the one sabotaging me." He stepped into her again then backed up one step. She loosened her body telling him that it was okay. He sat next to her on the couch.

"Where is Carson?"

"Do you really care?"

His hand reached towards her knee. "If you were mine, I would always be there for you." Jefferson paused then retracted his hand. Her knee bounced lightly. What was he really doing here? And why couldn't he ever give her a straight answer. The man infuriated her, but there was something about him that drove her crazy.

"You don't miss me." The couple's eyes met.

"Are you sure?" He reduced the empty space between them. Ebony wanted to move, but the small couch didn't allow that and neither did her legs. She could smell the spices on his breath guessing that he ha eating some spicy food recently. His pointer finger rose lightly grazing her ear lobe. Ebony leaned into his touch. He dragged his finger down her cheek, tracing her chin.

Her fingers tingled as she clinched the sides of the couch cushions. Jefferson's finger moved to her bottom lip followed by the wetness of his tongue. He outlined her lips like a lip pencil before slipping his tongue into her mouth. Ebony returned the wrongful kiss letting her tongue meet his. As much as she didn't want to admit it, she missed this man. Jefferson put his hand on her bare knee running his hand up her thigh under the emerald colored fabric. His hand reached her womanhood.

"I see you have missed me too." He said after feeling the wetness that had formed.

Ebony grabbed his wrist pulling him out of her.

"I can't do this again." She jumped up making her way to the door. His breath warmed her neck through her hair. Her hand grasped the door handle jiggling it but she couldn't get it open. Jefferson took one hand running it up her neck into her scalp. Her shoulders dropped and her head rested on the door surrendering to his touch. His hand retracted from her head grabbing her hair at the same time pulling her head back up right. Jefferson circled his hand around her neck squeezing slightly. His free hand managed to lift her dress up resting it on her bottom.

"What a beautiful sight." His hand circled her ass before smacking it hard. Her weight shifted losing her balance but his grasp tightened around her neck straightening her back up right. Ebony closed her eyes enjoying every bit of the pleasure she was feeling. She heard his belt buckle come loose. Her wetness increased as her body braced for what was to come. Jefferson strong arms slipped her panties to the side. Within seconds his strong manhood was felt inside her.

"Oh God." She screamed out. His hand moved from around her neck up to her mouth. She grabbed his pointer finger inserting it in her mouth to suck on. The slow deep strokes were making it hard for her to stand. She braced herself against the door so she could take in all that he was giving to her. Ebony whimpered in pleasure missing this man even though he caused her so much distress in her marriage last year but the spontaneity of his love making was addictive. He knew exactly what her body needed and how to give it to her.

"Your body still responds well to me. I wish you would accept that." He whispered in her ear. Her body dripped with pleasure.

"Ebony, you okay?" A familiar voice said from the other side of the door.

"I'm coming." She hollered. Hearing Joe's voice brought her back to reality.

"Stop, I can't." She spoke quietly trying to get free from Jefferson.

"You already did. He quickened his pace, grabbed her waist and made her body convulse into maximum pleasure. Jefferson pulled out quickly. Ebony collapsed to the floor.

"I hate you. This was a mistake. What is wrong with me?" She spoke between breaths.

"I know you do, but you love me the same." Jefferson pulled his pants up. Ebony slid her body to the love seat to sit on. "Don't be hard on yourself. You are in a marriage with a man you love, but don't get the satisfaction you need. It's not your fault."

She cut her eyes at Jefferson remembering why she hated him so much.

"Get out please." He walked to her kissing her gently on the forehead before leaving the room. Ebony cleaned herself up changing her clothes. She did a final check in the mirror before returning to the club.

Ebony took the empty seat next to her best friend.

"You look flushed, you okay?" Melody asked her.

Ebony turned to her best friend, eye twitching uncontrollably.

"What happened?"

"I can't talk about it." She mouthed.

Melody stood up walking towards the bathroom, Ebony followed.

"Spill it Bitch." Her best friend demanded as she pushed open the large wooden bathroom door.

"He was here." Ebony whispered checking under the bathroom stalls.

"Who?" Ebony stood eyes wide like she had seen a ghost.

"No, not..." Melody's jaw dropped.

"And I gave into that man again. Or he kind of took it. I don't know." Ebony looked her best friend in the eye through the square bathroom mirror.

"Why does he touch me and kiss me the way my husband can't?"

"I miss all the juicy stuff. What are you going to do girl?"

Her eyes drooped. "I really don't know."

FIFTEEN

*C*arson walked through the door at six pm like always but to a different sight then usual.

"I'm home." India danced around the kitchen to Beyonce in a pair of leopard boy shorts and a white tank top that exposed her small nipples pointing straight ahead. Carson focused on the frying pan and the chicken that was browning in it. This situation did not look good. If his wife walked through the door right now, would she be okay with it? Or did it really matter since she went off to Atlanta with her best friend instead of her husband and hasn't even bothered to call once since she's been gone.

"Wine?" India took a sip of blush wine before handing the glass to her brother in law.

"Smells good. I miss a home cooked meal." Carson took a sip of wine and set the glass on the kitchen table.

"I hope you're hungry." She pulled a glass dish of scalloped potatoes out of the oven placing it on top of the burners.

"I'll be right back."

Carson went up stairs to change out of his work clothes. He grabbed a pair of sweat pants and a t- shirt. His cell phone vibrated. Ebony's name flashed across the screen. She said everything was good and she would be home in a few days. Her husband starred at the emotionless message. No I love you, I miss you, nothing. He tossed the phone on the bed and left the room. He still wasn't ready to deal with her right now. India had dished up his plate with two pieces of chicken, a hearty scoop of potatoes, string beans and a basket of buttered dinner rolls sat in the middle of the table.

"You out did yourself." commented Carson.

"You deserve it."

The two sat down eating their dinner in silence. Her IPod switched to Earth, Wind, and Fire. Carson ate his potatoes trying to remember the last time him and his wife had a romantic dinner. When they first got together, she would make candlelight dinners for him all the time and they would make love all night. His mind couldn't remember back to those times anymore. He rubbed his temple, worried about the future of his relationship.

"Dance with me." India stood to his side with her hand extended. Carson stood putting his napkin on the table knowing that none of this situation was right but he couldn't help but admit that he liked the attention. He took both of her hands, holding her at arms length. India grinned. She stepped into the open space between them wrapping his left hand around her lower back. She laid her head on his chest wrapping her arms around him. It felt good to be held and wanted, it was just the wrong sister. The song switched back to an up tempo song. Carson pulled back as his eyes looked down into India's. Her clear, smooth, mocha skin, perfectly shaped eye brows covering her long eye lashes; he had never noticed how beautiful she was. Then again he had never looked at her in a romantic way, it was just wrong.

Carson broke away, retiring to the living room. India grabbed the bottle of wine from the table and joined him on the floor in front of the couch. Carson stretched out. India took a long sip from the bottle before passing it up to Carson.

"What are you going to do with your life? You can't keep dancing." India dropped her head back onto the couch.

"You sound like my mother."

"She knows your dancing?" Carson lifted his head up.

"Well not that part, just the life part." He handed the bottle back to her.

"My sister is getting her wish, but what about me? I miss my dad giving me advice. I just feel so lost."

India took a long sip of wine then put her head down towards the floor. He had watched his wife walk around like she was the only one affected by her fathers death, but clearly it was tearing up the whole family. They needed each other to get through this. He just wished his wife would see that.

By the third bottle of wine, Carson had made his way on the floor as well. He was sloped down, leaning against the bottom cushion while India was all the way laid out on the floor starring at the ceiling.

"What kind of animal would you be?"

"What?" She giggled as she sat up.

"I would be a monkey or a bird then I could fly anywhere I want to and not be bothered by anyone, just free." The pain and sorrow left her eyes as she talked.

"I would be a lion, ferocious and strong, powerful and sleek." Carson took a sip from the bottle. He usually never drank this much.

"I think you're all that. You are strong and powerful. You don't have to be loud about it. It's your quietness that shows your strength." India got close enough to smell the alcohol coming from his breath. She grabbed the bottle and his hand. "And that's what I love about you, that's what makes you a great man."

Their eyes connected. Did she just use the L word? Carson shook his head slowly confused and dizzy at the same time. He was not a drinker and his limit was two bottles ago. India's head moved slowly towards his. She lowered the bottle resting the base on the carpet. Her hands cupped the lower part of his cheeks. Their lips connected. India leaned into the kiss straddling him at the same time. Carson's hands grabbed her small waist running up the sides of her body under her undershirt. India pulled back to take her shirt off. He looked her in the eye realizing who she was.

"I can't do this." He pushed her off his lap.

"She doesn't deserve you, or appreciate you. She's in hot lanta doing who knows what while your home being a good husband." Carson picked up the wine bottle to finish it off. He didn't feel like he was being a good husband and after her affair last year, he hoped his wife would not do anything to come between them again, but could he really trust her. She did it once, would she do it again? He starred at India who had taken off her bra and under shirt. Her nipples were begging to be sucked by the way they were pointing at him. He swallowed deep and wiped the extra saliva from the corners of his mouth. The empty wine bottle rolled on the carpet as Carson lay back down as the room starting spinning. He closed his eyes but the room spun more quickly. His eye lids opened slowly to see India pulling the string of his sweatpants. He rolled to the side and she pulled them down slightly. His lower half did not agree with his head. Before he knew it, he felt warm moisture on the tip of his manhood. His eyes rolled back into his head as he enjoyed a feeling that was long over due. His hands got wrapped up in her natural hair.

"Oh God." He hollered out. He opened his eyes. India had a huge grin on his face.

"Forgive me." Carson said. He sat up grabbing her by the waist, throwing her to the ground. His lips went straight for her perky nipples massaging them one at a time with his tongue. He pulled down her boy shorts taking note of her beautiful body. Deep down he knew this was wrong, but it felt so right he could not deny it. Carson slid into her as her nails dug into his back. She wrapped both legs around his waist squeezing tightly. He buried his head into her chest. He had missed that feeling for so long. He couldn't remember the last time he had such passionate sex. His strokes got longer and slower, not wanting the feeling to ever end. He felt squeezing on the head of his dick.

"Oh myyyyy." Carson let out as he exploded. He rolled over onto the floor starring at the carpet. He couldn't bring himself to look at her in the eye. He had just cheated on his wife and with her sister. What was he thinking? Ebony would not accept that he was drunk. That was no excuse for what he did.

SIXTEEN

———— ⟋⟍⟍ ————

"I'm home." Ebony hollered to what seemed to be an empty house. Her plane had touched down an hour ago and after unwillingly dropping her best friend off to her abusive husband, she made her way home. Even though she had only been gone for a weekend, she missed being home, but didn't miss the state of her house when she left. She was nervous to see her husband especially after what happened while she was away. As much as she wanted to deny it, there were more than just her and Carson in this marriage.

Ebony looked around the fairly clean kitchen. She spotted two wine glasses in the sink and several empty wine bottles in the trash can. Picking one up, she read the label. Carson never drank white wine. The side door opened behind her.

"Hello."

"Hi." Carson walked in walking right by his wife like she hadn't been away for a few days.

"How was your show?"

"Good thanks." He walked by her to the refrigerator. She didn't expect anything else from him but a hug or an awkward kiss would have been nice. Ebony had never felt more like a stranger in her own home. "Did you have a party?" She shook the wine bottle before returning it back to the trash. Knowing it wasn't his style but she was owed an explanation.

"Oh no." He laughed uncomfortably.

Ebony tilted her head to the side waiting for more, but got nothing.

"What do you want to do for dinner? I know you don't want to cook." Her husband asked. He went to the small drawer in the kitchen pulling out a stack of carry out menus.

"It doesn't matter. I don't have much of an appetite." Ebony took her small suitcase up stairs to unpack. The picture of her father was starring her in the face as she put her jewelry back in her jewelry box. She grabbed the picture frame taking a seat on the edge of the bed. If this wasn't a time for her father's advice, she didn't know what was. She needed advice on her marriage. The uncomfortable feeling that was downstairs was too much for her to handle. She was afraid if she had the conversation with her husband, then she would have to admit her indiscretion over the weekend and she wasn't ready to do that. The alternative, let things stay the way they were and hope their marriage gets better.

"I ordered Chinese." Carson said as he walked into the bedroom.

"That's fine."

The two of them changed their clothes in silence throwing on something more comfortable.

"What did you order me?"

"Fried rice of course. I know what my wife likes." He said blandly. Carson knew her like the back of his hand although it was strange how he didn't know she was cheating last year, or he knew and just didn't want to admit it to himself because he knew the consequences.

Ebony came to the front of the bed where Carson was putting on his socks. She knelt down in front of him.

"Are we ok?"

Carson stayed focus on his socks, never making eye contact.

"You left me a note to say you were going away, so you tell me."

He stood up walking to the dresser.

"Is this what our new life will be like? You on the road all the time and me left at home alone?" Her husband braced himself on the dresser leaning over. Ebony stood up following him. She put her hand on his shoulder. Their eyes met in the mirror. Words didn't come to her. What was she supposed to say that she would give up singing to be the devoted wife with no career or future? It was an unfair choice to have to make.

"A marriage is a compromise. Don't ask me to choose my happiness for our happiness." Her bottom lip quivered. Would Carson be able to support her in her new venture? This was a new life for her and she wanted his support. She just wasn't sure that he could do that.

A knock came from the front door breaking their stares.

"My wallet's on the counter." Carson leaned up letting his wife's hand fall off his back.

"I got it."

"Of course you do." Carson said silently under his breath. His wife's eyes lowered as she stormed out of the room. Now he had a problem with her making her own money? One more thing to add to the list of things Carson was unhappy about. How would she be able to make things better between them? Going back to her old life where he is the bread winner and she had no singing career was not an option so he would have to learn to deal with that. She couldn't help him with that.

"Hey homey." India's face dropped when she saw her sister at the door.

"Homey?"

"I didn't expect you to be home already."

Ebony looked at her sister in a short jean mini skirt and off the shoulder sweater.

"Sorry to disappoint you." India walked past her sister carrying a grocery bag. "Are you the one who helped him drink all that wine?"

"Is that what he told you?" Ebony looked at her sister sideways. Why was she acting weird?

"What's in the bag?"

"I thought your husband might be hungry." Carson appeared behind them. India looked at him with an apologetic look in her eyes. Ebony turned back to look at her husband who looked the same.

"I think I can feed my own husband." Who did she think she was? India was really showing off.

Carson stepped up. "Your sister just kept me company yesterday so I wouldn't have to eat take out again. It was nice to have someone cook for me."

"Hello." The Chinese delivery man was standing at the door. Ebony paid him and shut the front door with mix feelings. Was she being a bad wife by not cooking for her husband every night? Her life had taken a 360 and she has been very busy now while she is building her career and it will only get worse. But why can't she have the best of both worlds, should she really have to give up her career to be a stay at home wife?

Carson walked towards India taking the bag out of her hand.

"I appreciate the thought. Come eat with us. There is plenty of food."

Please say no. Ebony was not in the mood for her sister.

"Sure." India walked into the kitchen like her sister didn't exist. She had never had a problem with the relationship her husband and sister have had, but this was getting on her nerves.

Ebony twirled her fork through her friend rice feeling like a third wheel in her own house. She watched her sister and her husband talk about some movie they were watching the other night. She hadn't seen Carson laugh so much in months. India kept reaching over the table touching her husbands hand in a playful manor. Ebony rolled her eyes every time she did. He acted like they weren't just talking about the state of their marriage more then ten minutes ago.

"Must have been a great movie?" Ebony said sarcastically. The two stopped laughing and looked in her direction.

Ebony waved her hand in a drunken manner. "No please carry on."

She excused herself from the table grabbing some wine from the refrigerator.

"I don't know why dad loved you so much. You're a spoiled brat."

Ebony scratched her nails against the breakfast bar. "What did you say?"

Carson jumped up out of his seat. India rose slowly, eyes glaring at her sister.

"You don't cook for your husband. You go off being selfish leaving loved ones while you try to become famous. Mom is dying inside, he's unhappy and you're acting like a brat because he's happy for once. You don't deserve a man like him."

Ebony raised her head slowly, eyes burning.

"I worked for mom for years and now I want something for myself and I'm being selfish. You have some nerve." She whipped her head starring at her husband. "You feel this way?" He just sat motionless.

India got up walking towards her sister.

"I've always been there for this family while you've been the party girl. Now it's my time to have my fun and my own life."

"The world doesn't revolve around Ebony." India held her arms up. "Just be there for someone else." Carson snapped out of his trance jumping between the two females.

"You bitch." Ebony jumped towards her sister grabbing a hand full of her natural hair. India jumped back reaching over Carson's head swinging her hands in an uncontrolled manor. Carson slipped himself from in between so he could see both women.

"Let it go." He tried to peel his wife's fingers from her sister's hair. "I said let-her-hair-go." Ebony looked up at her husband, wide eyed. She had never heard him raise his voice. She let go of her sister's hair. India's hand landed right across her sister's right cheek. Carson grabbed his wife before she could retaliate.

"You're done. You over there. You there." He pointed to opposite sides of the house for the women to retrieve to. India grabbed her purse and let herself out the house. Ebony's husband glared at her with folded arms.

"What? Do you agree with her too? Are you unhappy?"

"I'm not getting into it Ebony."

"That's the problem, you never say anything and you don't have my back."

Her husband made two fists as he started pacing the kitchen.

"I'm not doing this with you." Carson grabs his keys, walking towards the door.

"That's right, go follow her." She threw her wine glass at the door shattering it.

SEVENTEEN

———— ⟨≈⟩ ————

*C*arson climbed on the tread mill, put his ear buds in his ears, and cranked it to full speed. Within minutes sweat was dripping down his face within minutes. After breaking up the fight between his wife and her sister, the only place Carson felt relief was at the gym. He had never wanted to be away from his wife so bad. The distance between them, the betrayal with his sister and not feeling like the man of his own house anymore was becoming too much. Ebony pushed him and he wasn't ready to say how he really felt to her for the fear that it might break their marriage.

"Slow down. You going to kill yourself and I'm not for going to the hospital tonight."

Carson removed his ear phones glaring at his best friend.

"Damn man, I didn't sleep with you last night."

Carson ran even faster, not being in the mood for Mike's smart ass. Mike reached out declining the speed on the tread mill to a walk. Carson stepped to the sides of the machine until it stopped completely. He walked over to the free weights. Mike followed.

"I can't do this."

Carson picked up 30 lb weights curling them rapidly.

"Ebony and her sister got into a fight, my wife is getting a career with no time for me, and some more shit."

Mike starred at him through the long mirror in front of them.

"What other stuff?" Carson never made eye contact even though he could feel his best friend starring at him.

"I made a mistake, a big one." Carson looked around. They were the only two in the weight area. "I slept with my wife's sister."

Mike's jaw dropped. "You did what? This is better then a movie."

"Shut up man." Carson looked around again to see who was starring at them. Carson explained his drunken night with India and how the guilt was killing him and he needed to come clean with his wife but didn't know how and after the fight they had, Ebony wouldn't forgive either one of them.

Mike laughed hysterically. "Where is my best friend, because this guy, I don't know him, but I like him?"

Carson walked away going into the locker room. Mike followed still laughing.

"I was walking away from you for you not to follow."

Carson opened his locker and a small piece of paper fell to the floor. He grabbed it as he sat on the bench. Mike stood next to him with one leg propped on the bench. His hand touched Carson's shoulder.

"What are you going to do man?"

"Is it selfish of me to want my wife to not have a fancy career, to be home for me?"

"If I were you, I would let her make the money and sit my ass home all day or follow her around the country, why not."

Carson rubbed his forehead. He opened the note that was still in his hand.

It read "You deserve better. Now you two must pay." He threw the paper in the air watching it drift back down to the floor. Mike picked it up and read it.

"Man, you got some shit going on with you."

"I know. My life use to be simple." Carson slipped off his tennis shoes and changed out of his gym clothes. "I need a drink."

The guys walked to the parking lot.

"What the..." Carson looked at his car which seemed to be leaning to one side. His two driver side tires were flat.

He lifted his hands to the sky.

"This is not my week. Why God, why?"

"I'll take care of this tomorrow. I don't feel like dealing with this tonight."

He jumped into the car with Mike who was supposed to drive him home, but made a stop in between.

"What are we doing here?" Carson frowned at the neon sign of the strip club. He prayed India was not working tonight. The club was fairly empty except for a few lonely old men.

"Two beers sweetheart." Mike ordered as they took a seat on two empty bar stools. Carson threw a two dollar bills on the stage at the young Hispanic girl who had just finished her set. India walked out on the stage next in a one piece sailor outfit with long white stockings on and very high heels.

"You're in big trouble." Mike commented as he looked from Carson to India. Her eyes locked in on Carson as she walked slowly in front of the stage pole swinging one leg slowly around it. She smiled devilishly at him. What was she thinking? She had just fought with her sister and was still flirting with Carson. She was begging for trouble.

India dropped to her knees crawling across the bar stage towards Mike. She lay in front of the two men swinging her legs in a circular motion showing what was under her dress.

Mike's hand crept up her leg. Carson's face turned red as he starred his friend down. He didn't want him touching her at all, but that was not his place to say so. India flirted right back guiding his hand to her chest area.

"Excuse me." Carson got up from the bar stool going outside to get some air. Something strange was going on with the notes and now his car. He knew they were related somehow. Maybe Ebony had been right about seeing Leslie at the wedding.

"What's wrong with you?" India asked appearing next to Carson.

"Nothing." He paced in front of the door.

India looked through the dark night trying to see if anyone else was outside with them. "Come on." She walked off towards the parking lot. Carson followed. They got into her car.

"I wanted to check on you after the argument."

"I'm not worried about my sister. She doesn't bother me."

Those two had such a strange relationship. Carson didn't care to try and figure it out tonight.

"I'd rather talk about us." India put her hand on Carson's knee. He looked her in the eye as he removed it.

"There is no us. We had a moment of …I don't know what it was, it just wasn't supposed to happen." He rubbed his forehead. This was too much drama for him. He was use to a nice peaceful life but since his wife has started her career, things have gotten crazy in his life and he didn't like all the excitement.

India leaned over sliding Carson's chair back. She climbed from the driver's seat and straddled him.

"What?" Her finger landed on his lips hushing him. She moved in close so the tips of their noses touched. The smell of alcohol filled the air. Her finger dropped and her lips brushed against his. Carson's heart rate rose, his breathing got heavy and the blood rushes to the lower half of his body. India had always been the cute, little sister, but until this moment, he had never noticed how much he really was into her. They always had a friendship, but maybe his feelings were more than friends.

Carson grabbed her inner thighs squeezing them tightly. India ran her tongue across his bottom lip before kissing him deeply.

"What are we doing?" He pulled back looking into her big, brown eyes for answers. There was a calming, sweetness in her eyes unlike his wife's that only seemed to have anger and determination lately, not love for him. He loosened his grip raising his hands in the air.

"You need to relax." India whispered as she unbuttoned the button on his pants.

His hand grabbed her hair forcefully pulling her head up. His eyes quickly moved back and fourth looking for something to stop him from making another huge mistake. India grabbed his ears rubbing them gently. He pulled his hands closer to his face bringer her head in with them kissing her forcefully. She returned the kiss.

The windows fogged up making it hard to see out the car and harder for anyone to see in. His hands ran up her slender back lifting the short sailor suit up. India grabbed his dick from his pants. She moved back to the driver's seat. Carson leaned back in the seat closing his eyes. He felt the wet, warmness from her mouth on his man parts. He let out a moan missing the feeling. India licked him slowly then quickly. She sucked gently then lightly, blowing on his penis causing several sensations. His eyes rolled back into his head. He grabbed her shoulders losing all composure. India was grinning as he opened his eyes. She slid over lowering herself down on his still hard dick.

"Oh" He squeezed her waist tightly helping to regulate the speed of her pulses. His eyes closed again focused on the pure pleasure he was feeling, not the pain he was causing or the betrayal to his wife. India rode him slowly, then fast, and slow again. She placed one hand on the window to steady her and held his shoulder with the other. His body trembled. Carson lifted India from off him as he exploded. Things happened so quickly that he didn't have time to use a condom. India handed him a stack of napkins from the glove box and moved back to her seat. She grinned.

"What's so funny?" Carson asked.

"That's a lot", she looked down at her work. "It's nice to see you satisfied and relieving all this stress."

"India." He said firmly. "We have to stop doing this. It's not right and it's just going to hurt everyone."

He balled up the napkins looking for a place to put them. She pulled out a plastic shopping back from the back seat opening it for him. His eyes widened. Was she planning this moment all along? He didn't put it past her. India laughed leaning over to kiss him again. Carson grabbed her face stopping her.

"I'm serious India. I've let this get too far and it's my fault, but it stops now."

He stormed out of the car and joined Mike back inside the club. Carson never turned back around hoping India would get the message. Now he just had to stick to his end of the bargain.

EIGHTEEN

———————— ⚮ ————————

"This is a surprise." Jefferson opened the door letting Ebony in. After her husband had stormed out, she didn't want to stay home and think about what had just happened. She got in her car and ended up at his place. She needed answers.

"You're looking casually fine." She looked down at her black leggings and fitted t-shirt.

"Thanks." She said slowly. He was still wearing work clothes. A pair of gray dress pants, a button up shirt with the first three buttons open and his tie loosened, hanging from his neck.

"Just getting off work?" She asked walking into the house.

"I had a late meeting." She could feel his eyes watching her, but didn't hear footsteps behind her. She turned back and he was still at the door looking at her puzzled.

"Why are you looking at me like that?" She stooped in the hallway.

"Why are you here? You seemed mad with me in Atlanta." He walked towards her slowly with his hands in his pockets. Ebony looked to her left spotting a picture of Jefferson and Leslie on the wall. That was his downfall that he was related to that nut job of a sister.

"I really don't know." She continued to his couch, kicking off her shoes and sitting Indian style. As much as she loathed him, she always felt like herself around him. He didn't judge her or ask a bunch of personal questions that she didn't want to answer. Maybe he didn't care about her personal life, but right about now that's all she wanted.

Jefferson stood over her.

"I'm sorry for interrupting your night. I just couldn't be home right now."

"It's fine. I'm going to take a shower. There's some pasta on the stove if you're hungry."

"Hey, have you talked to your sister? There's some things going on that can't be explained and if it's not you, then it has to be her."

"I visit her once a week. She doesn't even talk about you two any more. She really is doing better." She rubbed her hand against her chest hoping he was telling the truth.

Jefferson walked towards the stair case taking off his shirt exposing his muscular back as he turned the corner walking up the steps. Ebony shook her head at his incredible body. Her insides tingled as she felt moisture in her panties.

"That man is so irresistible."

She walked to the kitchen peeking into the pot of spaghetti noodles with peas, carrots, and some other vegetables mixed in. She sampled it impressed by his skills. This man had it all except for his ego. He was a great catch. If only she had met him before her husband. She could hear the shower. Ebony crept up the steps slowly hoping they didn't creek. She wanted to see his body in all its glory nice and wet. She felt like a school girl sneaking around as she peeked through his cracked bathroom door. Jefferson stood in the mirror butt naked, starring at his physique before stepping into the shower. Ebony grinned. She backed up from the door thinking of her husband wondering what she was doing in this mans house again. Didn't she learn anything from the affair last year? It was in this same house where Leslie had tried to kill her and the truth of their pasts had come out. She looked to his king size bed half made up; so much pleasure at this place and so much pain.

"What am I doing here?" She whispered to herself.

"You don't have to lurk outside the door." Ebony covered her mouth. How does she always get caught by him? He had some type of sick sense that drove her crazy. She stepped into the bathroom sitting on the toilet seat.

"Are you happy with your life?"

He pulled back the shower curtain looking at her. Soap was lathered all over his body. Ebony licked her lips as she watched soap drip from his well endowed member.

"What's there to be unhappy about? With a body like this, a face like this, and I'm single to fuck anyone I want. Yes I'm happy. You should be too. Your life is changing and your dreams are finally coming true." He shut the shower curtain. "You stay on track; you will be a huge star."

"I guess." She said slowly looking down at the toilet. He made it sound so much better than it really was. Even if she became rich and famous, what would it cost her?

"Come get a hug." She lowered her eyes. Did he want her to join him in the shower?" She didn't come here for that, but …

Ebony crossed her legs and grabbed her chin. The image of her husband running after India pissed her off. She knew he wasn't doing anything as bad a she was, but he still should have kept his butt in the house.

Ebony slipped out of her clothes, pulled back the shower curtain and stepped in. Ebony felt herself turning into her best friend. She couldn't understand what possessed her to keep doing this stuff except for the feeling of lust that she had towards this man and the incredible sex that she wasn't getting at home.

Jefferson handed her the wash cloth over his shoulder. She gently massaged his massive muscles squeezing them. Her hands continued down his back to his hard ass. Wrapping her hands around his waist, she laid her head on his back needing to feel the comfort of a man. Jefferson turned around giving her a proper hug. His hard member rested on her leg turning her on. His arms wrapped around her waist lifting her up. Her legs hugged him tightly. He turned her around putting her under the water. She loosened the grasp around his neck giving her some space between them. Ebony slid him inside and bounced up and down riding him. Jefferson moved his hand to under her butt. She watched his muscles flex as he supported her weight. Carson is not strong enough to do this even with all the time he spends at the gym.

"I can't do this." Jefferson said putting Ebony down. She cocked her head to the side. He had never turned her down. Jefferson turned the water off and stepped out the shower.

"Are you serious? You practically raped me in Atlanta and now you don't want to have sex with me."

He chuckled which made her even madder. Jefferson stepped out of the shower, cradled her in his arms carrying her to his bed. He put a towel down then laid her down on it. Her naked body glistened from the water droplets. Ebony covered her face. His body blanketed her as his lips encompassed her breasts. She giggled as his tongue swirled around her nipples. She rubbed his bald head having the time of her life. As Jefferson came up for air, he looked at her in the eyes with a look she had never seen before. He was serious. Her whole body throbbed, especially between her legs. She needed to feel him inside her but he looked like he had something on his mind.

"What is it?" She cupped his face.

"I really enjoy being with you." Her heart melted hearing that from him. Their lips met half way. She kissed him deeply bringing him all the way down to the bed. Her legs wrapped him as he dove in; long, slow, deep strokes. Ebony could feel him in the pit of her stomach. Her nails dug deep into his back embracing all the pain that he was giving to her.

"I love being with you." She whispered in his ear before nibbling on it. Jefferson braced himself on his knees, freeing his ear from her lips. He bent her legs up pounding her quick and hard.

"Oh Gosh." She shouted out as her body exploded several times.

"Stop, please stop." She begged him not being able to take any more.

He stopped moving starring down at her. "You want me to stop?"

She shook her head, eye twitching. Jefferson moved slowly teasing her.

"You want me to stop, beg me." His motions started slowly, and then he picked up his pace, faster and faster. Ebony let out a series of loud screams before ripping the sheets from the bed to stuff in her mouth. Jefferson laughed through gritted teeth as he came. He collapsed on the bed right next to Ebony. His watch on the night stand read eleven thirty pm. Ebony wondered if her husband was still out in the streets or if had came home. If he was home then she would have to think up a lie to where she has been. Before she could use the restaurant, but since she didn't work there anymore, that was out. She couldn't say she was with her mom because he could double check that story with India since she was staying there right now. Melody was her best bet; she would always lie for her.

Ebony got up to go wash up. Jefferson had drifted off to sleep. She got dressed and crept down the stairs to check her cell phone. If her husband had text her, then she would have to think up a lie. If he hadn't he was probably still out. Her phone had ten missed calls and several text messages.

Her mother had called her, Carson called her several times, and a strange number had left a voice mail. She read the text messages.

"Oh my gosh." Her phone fell out of her hand as she read that her sister was in the hospital. She grabbed her things and darted for the door. As she sped down the road, she tried to call her husband back but he wouldn't answer the phone.

"Come on." She beat on her steering wheel in anger. "Why isn't he answering?"

What could have happened to her sister? This family couldn't take any more tragedy.

"Please God; don't let it be something serious. I can't lose her too, especially after our fight."

Ebony ran through the doors of the emergency room. She didn't recognize anyone in the waiting room. The nurse at the desk opened the double doors and told her where to go. She walked up the room five where her mother and husband where sitting on either side of the hospital bed. Her sister was lying on the bed, eyes closed with tubes coming out of her nose.

NINETEEN

Ebony walked into the hospital room two hours after the first phone call her husband had made to her. Carson could understand the hesitation of her not answering his calls, but her own mother's calls didn't make sense. Her hair was frizzy and matted like when she lets it dry wet. Looking out the small window into the dark sky Carson didn't see any rain drops on the window. It had been dry for days.

He narrowed his eyes at her from across the room. She made eye contact but quickly looked away. Something was definitely up.

"What happened?" Carson parted his lips but nothing nice would have come out so he said nothing.

"Someone attacked your sister." Her mother spoke.

"What? Where?"

"She was outside of some club. I don't know." Mrs. Lovely looked as disoriented as her daughter. She had on a pair of dark sweat pants which she never wore and a long wrinkled t-shirt that was big enough to be her husbands. Mrs. Lovely was always dressed nice, even on a casual day she looked like she had her work clothes on. The whole family was a mess these days.

"Where's the doctor, what are they saying?"

Ebony paced the room asking for answers. Carson rolled his eyes at his wife. She had some nerve to come in here with no explanation on where she's been or what she had been doing. If she would have been here early she could have talked to the doctor herself.

"She's fine." Carson talked slow and quiet. "They want to keep her for observation overnight but the person just shattered her window and she hit her head and got cut by the glass but they didn't actually attack her."

Ebony stopped walking to stare at her husband who hadn't let go of India's hand since she's been there. Ebony gave Carson a sideways glance.

"I've been here for hours." He explained.

"Were you with her?" Ebony's voice rose slightly.

"No", His voice was cold.

"She may not want to see you when she wakes up. It might upset her again."

His wife looked like she had just been slapped in the face. She looked to her mother for confirmation but she said nothing. Ebony slowly walked into the hallway letting the bright light from the hallway flash on her sister's face.

"What is going on?" Mrs. Lovely leaned over her sleeping daughter towards her son in law.

"They had a fight earlier today so everyone is on edge."

Their mother put her head down on the bed. "I don't know what to do anymore." She mumbled. Her head rose slowly, "I need to get myself together, if not for me, for them."

Carson reached his free hand across the bed placing it on top of Mrs. Lovely's hand. Tears fell from her eyes, probably still mourning her husband and now her daughter. Carson could see how painful this was for her. He hated seeing this family that had always seemed so put together on the outside in such turmoil. As a young boy he would spent so much time at the Lovely household because it was always a happy place to be. Now there was no more joy anywhere and his life was a mess as well so he didn't know how to put theirs back together.

"What's going on?" India opened her eyes speaking slowly.

"Hey you?" Carson and Mrs. Lovely both focused on India. She looked down at her brother in laws hand on hers then back at him. Carson moved his hand quickly.

"I'm going to get the doctor." Carson walked into the hall almost tripping over his wife's leg that was stretched out as she sat on the hospital floor outside her sister's room.

"What are you doing?"

"Waiting since you kicked me out."

Carson stepped over her walking to the nurse's station. He returned with a nurse. Carson let her enter the room alone as he looked at his wife. He wanted to slump to the floor with her, hold her, and discuss life like they use to do in college, but that bond has been broken. He wanted to repair it, but he just broke all rules and there was no turning back from that, but he has loved this woman his whole life and no matter what, he always will.

Carson reached his hand out helping her off the dirty floor. They walked into the room together. India looked at her sister, smiled slightly like she was up to something. Carson could hear his heart beating. He put his hand on his chest and took a seat in the plain brown plastic chair in the corner. She wouldn't say that they slept together in front of everyone would she? She probably would, just to get back at her sister. Oh my gosh. There was no way to talk him out of this. This would definitely end his marriage.

India parted her lips. Sweat droplets formed on his forehead. Carson inhaled deep

"I'm sorry for what I said earlier." He let his breath out with a puff.

"Me too." Ebony rushed to her sister grabbing her hand.

India winked at Carson and flashed him a smile as she hugged her sister. She was definitely up to something.

TWENTY

"Mom, what can I do?" Ebony turned to her mother as she pulled up in the driveway at the Lovely household. It had been a long restless night at the hospital. Between Carson, her mother, and her self, they all took turns sleeping on the couch. No one wanted to leave until India had been discharged with a clean bill of health except for a few scratches and cuts.

Her mom turned to her, the sun light illuminating her face, "You can't fix me baby. I just need time to heal in my own way." Her mother leaned over kissing her daughter on the forehead before getting out of the car. Ebony watched her mother enter the house before pulling off. Carson took India home so she had some time before he got home. She drove thirty minutes from town pulling up a long drive way. Her car winded the narrow road and up a small hill. She parked her car making the rest of the trip on foot. Ebony sat down next to the gray headstone, leaning against it.

"Hey dad, I miss you so much. We all do. I just don't know how to get along without you. Please tell me what to do? What would you say to me right now?" She leaned back on the headstone looking up at the cotton ball clouds. They moved quickly through the sky with peaks of sunlight flashing through. The only thing she wanted was to hear her father's stern, but comforting voice. He would put his arm around her as they swung on the porch swing, then he would say "follow your dreams and your heart and if no one likes it then tough. It's Ebony's world and you deserve everything out of it." Her eyes welled up with tears that couldn't be contained. Through her blurry vision she saw a white tissue waving in her face.

"Thank you." Ebony took the tissue from her best friend.

"Carson called." Ebony smiled. Her husband always knew what she needed even if he couldn't give it to her. Melody sat down joining her friend on the cool, spiky grass. She opened her arm letting Ebony lean into her. She closed her eyes being able to exhale all her current problems out. The two best friends sat as the sun set never speaking a word but that's exactly what Ebony needed, someone that knew her so well knew that words would ruin the moment.

Ebony opened her eyes to the night sky.

"Now what?" Melody spoke softly. Her best friend leaned up, stiff from leaning on her side.

"I don't know." Sadness resonated from her voice.

"Well were in a cemetery at night. It's kind of creepy." The two friends laughed picking themselves up from the ground.

"Next time can you end up at a bar? I'm starving." Melody said as they reached their cars.

"I need to go home." Melody hugged her best friend kissing her on the forehead.

Ebony pulled into the driveway. The night sky was as dark as the house. She slipped into the bed trying not to wake her husband. His hand wrapped around her waist as soon as her head hit the pillow. He probably couldn't sleep as well.

"You get India home safe?"

He mumbled something that sounded like yes. His grip tightened around her as his lips warmed her neck with light kisses.

"How was she?"

"I don't want to talk about her." He whispered in her ear before nibbling it. His other hand slipped between her legs; gentle at first but then became rough and more forceful. Ebony looked over her shoulder wondering who the stranger was in her bed. He slipped her panties off rubbing bare skin against bare skin. His next move would be to turn her over and do it missionary position, but he never did. Her husband slid in from behind with slow, long strokes. Ebony's mind raced. She didn't like the fact that she had been with Jefferson earlier and now her husband, it made her feel dirty, but she couldn't tell her husband no without a good reason. She wrinkled her forehead as her husband made love to her from behind. In all their years he had never done that. His love making was always predictable which made her wonder.

TWENTY-ONE

The crash of thunder shook the house waking Carson with a jolt. He rolled over extending his arm to grab his wife, but all he felt were cold, empty sheets. Rubbing his eyes, he spotted his wife sitting in the window seat focused on the rain. He laid back down rubbing his forehead thinking of the crazy weekend they had. When he dropped India off the day before, she swore to keep their little secret although Carson couldn't trust that she would do that. When they were teenagers, India use to get mad at her sister and tell her parents every time Ebony would sneak Carson into the house in the middle of the night. Her vengeance towards her sister might get the best of her again. His choice was to trust her or tell his wife on his own.

"What's on your mind?" He asked his wife who still hadn't moved.

"I was just thinking. So much has happened the past few days that I forgot my single release party is Friday. I don't feel prepared." She pulled her knees into her chest looking lost. He wanted to tell her how he really felt. That he thought this music stuff might be too much for her and although she has wanted this since she was younger, doesn't necessarily mean she was meant to do it. He didn't feel like fighting anymore so he kept his mouth shut.

"You will be fine." Ebony turned from the window glaring at her husband. I guess he said the wrong thing.

"That's it." The fight was coming weather he wanted to or not. Nothing he said or did lately seem to be right.

"Ebony, I don't know what you want me to say. You choose to pursue a music career in your thirties, you were unhappy with your life, and now you are second guessing yourself, I'm supposed to baby you, well I'm not." Carson sat up in the bed waiting for the back lash.

"I just wanted a little support and reassurance. I guess that was too much to ask for." Her voice was low and soft. Carson felt bad for going off on her like that, but he didn't regret what he said.

"Do you have plans today?" He tried to change the subject.

"I guess I need to practice some more." Ebony stood up and walked into the bathroom shutting the door behind her.

"I'm not happy." Carson said quietly once he heard the shower running. He laid back down curling in the fetal position.

....

Carson got out of the bed once the coast was clear. He watched his wife throw on a pair of jeans and a fitted t-shirt before leaving to meet up with Joe. There was a time, not too long ago when him and his wife use to spend the weekends together going out to eat or to the movies or just enjoying each others company, but now they were so far from that.

Carson turned the television on with nothing to do all day. He heard the doorbell ring. As he looked out the bedroom window at the driveway, he saw India's car. He shook his head knowing he shouldn't open the door, but he did.

"Your sister's not here."

"Good. I didn't come to see her." India smiled as she stepped past Carson. He turned to go up stairs and put some pants on because he just had his boxers and a white undershirt on.

"Need some help?" Carson jumped.

"I didn't hear you behind me." He could feel India's breath on his neck. "Let me help you." She grabbed his boxers at the waist pulling them down. He quickly tried to pull them back up.

"What are you doing?"

She smiled through her scars.

"I missed you all night so I waited for my sister to leave so I could see you."

Carson got free from her grasp moving to the bed to sit.

"I told you we can't do this again." He crossed his legs and folded his arms.

India walked slowly towards him. She uncrossed his legs with her hands and stepped in between.

"Remember when we were younger." He knew exactly what she was talking about. When Carson had bought the engagement ring, he asked India if her sister would approve. She begged him not to propose, she had confessed her love for him. Carson brushed it off and told her that Ebony was his soul mate; he never thought of the conversation again.

"The other night just proved that there is chemistry between us and you know it."

Carson knew it and the rest of his body knew it too but that would mean giving up on his wife and his marriage.

India leaned in making a connection with their lips. He leaned his head in then pulled it back. There eyes met as he shook his head no.

"For once, be bad."

"I have been bad and horrible to my wife." Carson put his head down.

"You think she's a saint?" He popped his head up quickly. What did she know that he didn't? Had Ebony been cheating again right under his nose? It would make sense why she was late to the hospital and when she went out of town was it really for business? Carson's head was spinning with questions. He loved her to death and forgave her once, but could he possible do this again. He deserved so much more.

India's chilly finger tips slipped in the hole in his boxers pulling out his manhood. Carson shifted. He instantly got warm as her lips covered his dick.

"India no, please don't do…this."

He leaned back onto the bed he shared with his wife just a few hours ago. He could still smell the sex on the sheets. His mind was full of questions, thoughts, regrets.

"Relax." Her voice was soothing. He took a deep breath giving into the feeling.

"That's it." She coached him. He could feel himself getting harder. He couldn't remember the last time his wife had bestowed this favor on him; how he had missed this. Her rhythm got quicker and wetter. Carson grabbed the sheets not being able to contain his self anymore. He opened his eyes feeling defeated. India stood up smiling as she wiped her lips.

"I told you."

She cut him off. "But your body told me something else. I know what you need? You need to come out of your shell." India pulled her dress off over her head exposing a pink lace bra and panty set. He instantly got hard again.

"I'm not that guy."

"For once you should be." India looked deep into his eyes. He didn't know what she was hoping to find.

"I'm not trying to be vengeful. I really care for you, I have for years, and you know that."

From valedictorian to designated driver, he has always been the good, responsible one. It's not like he hadn't already gone there with her and it was so good. What's one more time?

He grabbed his sister in law by the back of her neck, pulling her face into his. Her tongue slipped into his mouth wetting his lips as she pulled it out.

"Damn." He always made gentle love to his wife never wanting to be wild, but India's youth and sexuality brought something out of him that couldn't be explained. Carson lifted her body up, laying her on her back. He lifted her legs to his waist stepping in between them. He slid in slowly, enjoying the way her insides hugged him tightly.

"Oh." He grabbed her legs tighter getting his rhythm going. Carson turned to his right seeing his reflection in the mirror.

"What am I doing? I can't stoop to her level if she is cheating on me." His motions stopped as his head dropped. India reached up grabbing his chin.

"Focus on me." Her words were calming. Carson's eyes glazed with tears. Sitting up fully, India pulled his lips to hers kissing him deeply. She pulled him on top of her somehow knowing what he needed. Her legs wrapped tightly around him as he made deep passionate love to her.

The two lay enter twined in each other.

"I have no words." Carson smoothed her natural hair down with his hands. Although that was incredible, it didn't take away from the horrible feeling sitting in his gut. India has always had a tiny place in his heart and now she was filling up more than that.

TWENTY-TWO

*E*bony grudgingly walked into the studio. Singing was the last thing on her mind right now. Nothing creative could come out of her today and the rain wasn't helping.

"Good morning sunshine?" Joe was showing nothing but teeth that morning.

"You don't look like sunshine." He continued on. "And I don't feel like it either." She flopped down on the swivel chair next to him and the mixer board.

"Your parties only a few days away. We need to get through this rehearsal and lay down the next track for the album."

"I know, I know." Ebony crossed her arms leaning back into the chair.

"What's wrong sweetie?"

"Life, men, family…shall I go on?" Her feet twirled her chair around in slow circles. She leaned her head back looking at the plain ceiling.

"Maybe you should start with wardrobe because I see nothing is going to get done right now."

She stopped moving the chair, slamming her hands down on the arm rests. He was right. Her mind kept circling on her fight with her husband, the thought that she could have lost her sister and the way the whole family treated her in the hospital. Everything was making her question her career. If she were to erase all that has happened over the last few months and go back to her old life, would all these relationships be repaired? And then there's always Jefferson lurking in the back of her heart.

Ebony got out of the chair walking down the hall, down two floors to the basement. Stacey, a thin, young white girl with thin glasses greeted her.

"I love it here." Ebony said as she looked at all the glimmering dresses.

"Let's find you something spectacular to blow this performance out the water."

Ebony followed her watching her loose blonde curls bump up and down. After an hour of trying on different dresses, Ebony had finally found the perfect one. Shopping without spending money was the best and Ebony was smiling by the time she reached the elevator.

"You look better." Ebony smirked at Joe. "Ready to work?"

Ebony shook her head stepping into the booth. They rehearsed her first single, *Lover Scorn,* which she is planning to sing at her single release party. Joe had written a beautiful song which she loved but she couldn't wait until she was able to sing the songs she had written. Joe wanted her to start with a sure fire hit before they hit the people with her own stuff since she is new in the business.

Two hours later she stepped out of the booth to a small applause.

"Nice work. I'm taking you for a drink." Ebony smiled. "Let me check in." She grabbed her phone from her purse, no messages from her husband. She threw her phone back in.

"Let's go." They pulled up in front of a dingy looking bar with a neon sign.

"What is this place? I don't think I want anything they have." She turned her nose up at all the guys walking into the building.

"This place will get your mind off your troubles."

"I might find new troubles here, like herpes or something." She said pulling out a napkin from her purse to open the door with.

Joe laughed at her. Ebony's mouth dropped open as she stepped inside seeing a handful of half dressed women groping horny men. Joe grabbed her arm dragging her to the bar.

"Why are we here?" She took out her hand sanitizer, squirted it on a napkin, and wipe the bar stool with it before sitting down.

"You won't think about your problems here." She turned her nose up. "And it sounds funny but they have good food."

Ebony gave Joe a sideways glance.

"Come here often?" she asked.

"No, but it's a popular spot." Her head turned looking around at all the money handing from g-strings, boobs, and leg bands.

"Maybe I'm in the wrong line of work."

"Your money is definitely coming." The pair held up the small glasses of liquor that was put in front of them. She looked at the small stage to her right not interested in the plus sized girl with a cheap wig that needed to be straightened.

"What do you want to eat?" Joe asked sliding a menu in front of her. Ebony slid it right back.

"Is that...?" Ebony stood up walking slowly towards the stage. She stopped to the side standing behind a Caucasian man with a balding spot on the top of his head. She folded her arms and tapped her right foot. She starred intently at the young woman twirled herself around the stage. Ebony ran her fingers through her hair. No words could come to her mind. The dancer slunk to the ground crawling on the stage like a baby towards the bald headed man. She crawled slowly focused on him. Ebony stepped closer being able to smell his shampoo. Her eyes met her sisters who flashed a huge smile then winked at her. What the hell was India doing in a place like this and dancing of all things. Ebony stormed back to her bar stool.

"What's your problem?" She whipped her head around, eyes filled with fury.

"That's why you brought me here because of my sister?"

"What?"

Ebony pointed in the direction of the stage. "That's my sister."

"Oh wow." Joe looked past her to India. His eye brows rose. She put her hands in her face leaning on the bar. It all seemed like a bad dream that she couldn't shake. Ebony thought back to the bachelorette party when her sister was dancing the way she was and it all made sense but then it didn't. She sat back up taking both hands through her hair and putting it in a tight ponytail. Her sisters scratches hadn't healed all the way, but she felt she might get some new ones today. Her sister pranced over towards her wearing a proud smile like she had just won the Olympics.

"Hey sis." India leaned over the bar finishing her sisters drink. Ebony starred in awe.

"Hello." India leaned over towards Joe. She grabbed his face kissing him gently on the cheek. She ran her pointer finger down his round chin then over his lips. Ebony grabbed her sister's hand.

"Stop it. What is wrong with you?"

"My sister, she's so uptight." India leaned up against her sister's lap. Ebony put her hand on her sister's forehead. She starred into her sister's dilated pupils. Her makeup was so thick you could barely see her scratches.

She pushed her sister off of her. "Put your clothes on. I'm taking you home." Ebony's brown skin turned red.

"I'm working. Not everyone has talent like you." Her sister twerked as a guy walked by putting a dollar bill in her g-string then smacked her ass.

"Oh my gosh." Ebony looked up at Joe desperate for help but he was smiling at her ass as well. If Carson were here, he would carry India out of here. Ebony rolled her eyes. The bar tender put a plate of wings in front of Joe. Ebony grabbed one of the hot wings, took a big bite chewing hard. She thought about hitting her sister on the head with the empty bone but that wouldn't hurt her. Ebony threw the empty bone down and clinched the bar. Her body got warm and tingly. She had never been so mad at her sister. This was degrading to her and the family. How could she be a star and her sister be a stripper? The media would crucify her.

"I'm calling Carson. He will talk some sense into you." Ebony grabbed her phone from her purse.

"I'm surprised he's not here." India leaned in to her sister stumbling. Ebony moved her head back. "He does like to come here often and watch me." India touched herself all over. Ebony's eyes got big and her mouth opened wide. Did he know about this? He better not had kept this secret from her. That would be the ultimate betrayal.

"I can't." Ebony grabbed her purse storming out of the bar. She paced in the dusty parking lot hoping Joe would come out since he drove and she didn't know where she was. Her phone vibrated in her hand. It was a police officer trying to reach India. Ebony lied saying that she was her. He told her that they checked the cameras from the parking lot and ran the plate from the car of the person that tried to attack her. The car was under the name Jefferson. Ebony's hand shook as he talked. The door to the club pushed open and she dropped her phone. Joe walked to her picking the phone up.

"You look like you've seen a ghost." He handed the phone to her. "I mean I know that was a shock," he pointed towards the door, "you okay?"

"I just have to go." She walked to the passenger side of the car waiting to be let in. The ride back to the studio was silent. Ebony's leg bounced with the rumbling of the car engine. She couldn't wait to get out the car, she just didn't know who to confront first, but someone was going to give her answers.

"Do you want to postpone the party?" Joe broke her thoughts. "I see you have a lot of personal stuff going on."

A tear formed in the corner of her eye. That was the last thing she wanted but she didn't want all this stuff to affect her performance either. She had to make a decision. She was either all in, having nothing stand in the way of her dreams or she needed to hang it up now. She was too old and would not have another chance like this again.

"Can I have a day and I will let you know?" Joe parked the car.

"Sure." He said sadly. Ebony rubbed her forehead. She hated disappointing people.

Ebony got in her car and sped to her first destination. Her car screeched to a halt in front of Jefferson's town house. The light in the kitchen was on. She prayed that he didn't have company but she needed answers and couldn't wait until morning.

"You need to start calling first." Ebony pushed past Jefferson who was still in his work suit. She stopped right in the hallway pushing the door shut behind him.

"Did you come after my sister?"

"What? I don't know your sister."

Ebony walked in small circles. "The car was registered to you."

"Was it my truck?" She stopped pacing.

"I don't know." She shouted. "Why would you ask that? What are you hiding?"

Jefferson turned his back and walked off leaving her standing in the foyer alone. Ebony made two fists and stomped into the kitchen after him.

"Don't turn your back on me." She felt her face turn red.

He turned around quickly looking like he was going to hit her. "Don't you come into my house making accusations." He pointed his finger in her face. Ebony took a step back a little afraid of his anger.

"Don't you mess with my family. You put my sister in the hospital. She could have died. What the hell?"

His steps got closer backing her into the refrigerator. He grabbed her by the ponytail pulling her head back. She grabbed his hands trying to get free.

"I said I didn't do it." He talked slow and steady. She was paralyzed by his glare. Tears filled her eyes as her hair pulled from her scalp.

"You are hurting me." She whispered. His grip loosened. She bent over rubbing her head. Once she composed herself, she stood, furious. Ebony walked to him landing her hand across his right cheek.

"Don't ever do that again." His chest swelled up like the incredible hulk. Ebony's legs felt like jello. She had never seen him so mad. She wondered if this was such a good idea.

She squeezed her eyes shut tightly as he grabbed her by the shoulders twirling her around, lifting her and putting her on the counter top. He grabbed her face tightly pulling it close to him. She opened one eye then the other. There lips met forcefully. Her legs wrapped around him as she unbuttoned his shirt ripping it off of him. Her hands moved lower working on his pants. He grabbed her under her butt lifting her in the air. He shuffled to the living room with his pants around his ankles. He threw her on the couch taking his clothes all the way off as she worked on hers. Completely naked he sat down on the couch next to her. He patted his lap baiting her to sit on top. Ebony licked her lips as she saw how much he wanted her. She straddled his man hood lowering her body slowly down. She grabbed his broad shoulders helping to steady her as she rode him slowly. Jefferson slid down some on the couch positioning his feet on the floor. He grabbed her ass again giving it back to her. She cocked her head back taking in all the pleasure. The rhythm became quicker as Jefferson smacked her ass three times before releasing.

"I was not expecting this." Ebony said as she stood to her feet going to the bathroom to wash his scent off her before she went home. Ebony starred back at herself in the small powder room mirror. The cheating had become second nature to her and the fact that she wasn't feeling that bad about it anymore was troubling.

When she returned to the living room, Jefferson was still sitting naked motionless.

"You never answered my question from earlier?" She said not being distracted by his sex anymore.

He cleared his throat looking nervous. "I have several cars in my name for work." He spoke quietly. "I can check on them. Make sure none were stolen."

"I would appreciate that."

"This was not Leslie if that's what you're thinking."

"Are you sure? I feel like I've seen her and there is too much happening that can't be explained."

Ebony grabbed her chin. "It makes sense that it would be her." She thought about the letter to her house and the possible Leslie citing at the wedding but it still didn't make sense why someone would want to hurt her sister.

"I'm sorry."

Jefferson stood up grabbing his boxers. "I'm sorry about your sister."

Ebony kissed his cheek. Such a hard man, but inside there was a sweet spot deep down. She headed to the front door to have her second confrontation.

TWENTY-THREE

*C*arson looked out the window at the night sky. The clock on the night stand read ten pm. It was very late and he was surprised that Ebony was not home yet, but relieved because he was still cleaning up from his sister in law being in their bed. How could this have happened? To have sex with his wife's sister in their own bed; this whole situation was insane. Head lights shined on the opposite bedroom wall. Carson ran around the room spraying Lysol hopping that the scent of India was not left lingering in the room. He ran down the stairs to meet his wife in the kitchen. He wanted to make his marriage better, but he couldn't do it alone. He and Ebony were not on the same page. He wasn't happy but was his wife willing to change that? Even if they weren't vibing, he wanted to keep the piece in the house hold. He held his breath not knowing what to expect from his wife these days.

"Hi, how was your day?" He greeted her with a forced smile.

She threw her purse down on the breakfast bar then glared at him. He stepped back thinking smoke might come from her ears. He watched her go to the cup board, grabbed a small glass filling it with water drinking the whole thing without breathing.

"Did you know my sister was stripping?" She placed the glass down softly. His eyes widened as he tried to swallow the knot in his throat. Lie or tell the truth? How much does she know?

"I saw her there." *Damn it.* "She let on like you have been there to see her." Ebony crossed her arms under her chest.

Carson rubbed his forehead. "It wasn't my place."

"You are my husband." Her voice got louder as her hands went in the air.

"I told you to check on your sister."

"Don't turn this on me." Carson stepped out of the small space they called a kitchen. Ebony turned his direction slamming her hands on the counter.

"I can't do this; the lying, the deceit. I'm supposed to be living my dream right now, but instead everything and everyone around me is falling apart." Her chest heaved quickly. "You put my sister's life in danger with that crazy bitch."

Carson looked at her like he had just been slapped in the face. "What are you talking about?"

Ebony's eyes grew big like she exposed too much. She turned her back so she didn't have to look him in the eye.

"WHAT are you talking about?"

"Leslie." She sounded defeated.

He threw his hands in the air. "Your obsession with her is getting ridiculous."

Her lips were moving but no sound was coming out. Her eye twitched uncontrollably and he knew she was hiding something.

"Leslie was driving the car. The car was registered to Jefferson and it wasn't him. She attacked India."

Carson felt all the blood rush to his face. He grabbed the glass off the counter chucking it against the wall. Ebony flinched. That name brought out anger in him that he didn't know existed. He took a deep breath not wanting to say the words that were about to come out of his mouth.

"Are you sleeping with him again? Is that what this is about?" She starred at him blankly. His wife created more space between them. She didn't have to answer him because he already knew that answer. She did it again. What an ass he was. For almost three decades he had loved this woman who had now cheated on him twice. His deception didn't seem so bad anymore except that it was with her sister. He took his fist putting it into the kitchen wall.

"Shoot." He leaned over grabbing his hand.

He starred her in her beautiful brown eyes that looked so apologetic. He didn't care. It was too late to be sorry if she were.

Carson stormed off to the bedroom. He needed to create space between them.

Ebony followed him standing in the doorway.

"I think it best that I leave." Her words fell on him like a pile of bricks. He braced himself on the bed before taking a seat. The room seemed to be spinning. Carson leaned over putting his head between his legs. He could see her feet walking around the room probably gathering her things. He sat up lying back on the bed. Was this what he wanted? Space, yes, but moving out? Not sure.

"Why did you change the sheets?" She pulled the covers back probably looking for her hair scarf she wears to bed.

"I ah spilled something." He couldn't even look at her. Carson was very strict on eating and drinking in the bed, hopefully she wouldn't question that in this harsh moment. When he finally looked in her direction, she had two duffel bags packed sitting by the door to the bedroom. Carson sat all the way up not knowing what to do. It felt like goodbye, not see you later. His eyes burned with tears and anger. She walked to him extending her hand. He starred at her empty hand not wanting to touch her but thinking this may be the last time that he did. He touched it standing up. She fell into his arms. He wished she would always be this vulnerable with him, but she wasn't that women anymore.

His wife pulled back leaving him with a light kiss on the cheek.

"I'll be in touch." She picked up her bags and was gone. Carson went to the window watching her car back out of the driveway. Where would she go? A hotel, her mom's, or was that an excuse to run back to Jefferson. He grabbed his shirt tugging on it. The pain from his heart was too much to bear. Carson dropped to the floor grabbing his knees tightly. Tears flowed down his face feeling defeated.

TWENTY-FOUR

—⚓—

*T*he sun burned her tired eyes as it peeped through the long yellow curtains of the twenty story hotel that she ended up at last night. Ebony put the pillow over her face not ready to face the world today. Today would be about her making some life decisions. She needed to figure out her marriage, career, and family issues and only one person could help her with that. Ebony texted her best friend to meet her later this afternoon, her husband letting him know she was okay but he never responded back. She knew he was hurt, but right now neither one of them were happy so this was best for both of them and now that he knew about Jefferson again, there would be no turning back. She also texted Jefferson, not that he cared but she wanted to let him know what happened and that she was sorry for the way she came to his house last night.

Ebony rolled over grabbing the binder on the desk to look at the room service menu. She ordered the biggest breakfast on the menu hoping the record label would pay for some of her stay. She flipped on the television scanning through the morning news, talk shows, and court shows. Twenty minutes later her breakfast was being wheeled into her room. After eating, she threw on a short maxi dress with a long sweater and a white pair of tennis. She walked five blocks to central park going towards the Boat House Restaurant and down by the water. Most of the afternoon was spent sitting on a rock in a secluded part of the park. She hugged her legs tucking her dress under them. She took out a note pad writing down all her thoughts and feelings, all her problems and any solutions she could come up with. The silence in the middle of the city was just what she needed.

Ebony looked at her watch realizing half the day had gone by. She quickly walked back towards the hotel just in time to meet her best friend. There was a small lounge one block from the hotel where they had planned to meet. The sun was starting to set as the lit the place with small candles sitting on the long black table clothes that covered every table. The walls were dark and the place was filled with couches along the walls and chairs on the other side of the tables, very romantic setting.

"Hey Bitch." Melody said grabbing her best friend before sitting down on the chair. "What's up? You look a mess." Ebony took her hand smoothing down her hair.

"Thanks." She looked at her best friend who seemed much better than last time. Her weave was freshly done, make up looked good, not like it was covering any bruises or anything, and her girls were hanging out wanting attention like before she got married.

"How's home life? He hasn't put his hands on you again has he?" Ebony leaned in.

"No, I left him." Ebony clapped her hands together.

"He just let you go?"

"There was a fight, but ultimately he didn't have a choice."

Ebony ordered a bottle of red wine for the table and some sushi.

"I left Carson." Melody almost fell out of her chair. "Well I guess I didn't leave him, were just getting some space from each other."

"You should have started with that before I sat down." Melody took a big gulp from her wine glass then pushed Ebony's in front of her.

Ebony started from the beginning telling her best friend about the fight her and India had, the accident, the strip club, confronting Jefferson and Carson.

"We need another bottle of wine." Melody flagged down the waitress.

"So what now?" She leaned on her elbows on the table.

"I don't know." Her bottom lip poked out. Melody reached across the table grabbing her friend's wrists.

"I love you and I love your family, but this is your dream. Don't walk away to repair your family. They need time to work through their own stuff but this is your moment to shine and you can't let that pass you by. You will regret it for the rest of your life." Ebony reached across the table grabbing her friends hand back. Melody was always her voice of reason besides her father. She knew she was right she just needed to hear it from someone else so she didn't look like she was being selfish.

"I love you." She squeezed her hand tightly. The server came to the table placing a drink down causing them to pull away from each other.

"This is from the gentleman over there." She pointed to a bald headed clean dressed man who of course was the last person she needed to see tonight. Melody waved him over before Ebony could stop her. Jefferson slid into the booth with her kissing her on the cheek. She was taken back by his show of affection in public.

"You ladies looked very intense."

"We were having a private conversation." Melody flashed her best friend a look. Ebony shrugged her shoulders a little annoyed that he was in their presence right now. She really wanted to talk to her best friend alone. Jefferson put his hand on her knee rubbing it lightly.

"I think I'll go." Melody stood up, leaned over the table kissing her best friend on the cheek, then left. Ebony tensed her lips. She would get her later for this. Clearing her head did not include seeing Jefferson.

"What are you doing here?" Ebony asked angrily.

"You text me earlier and I saw your location so I came to check on you. So you finally left poindexter?"

Ebony pushed him slightly. "Not funny."

"Go take off your panties." He whispered in her ear. She looked at him like he had two heads.

"No, we are in a very nice restaurant."

"You scared?" Jefferson gave her a sneaky smile that made her instantly wet. She slid out the booth returning panty less. Jefferson returned his hand to her leg this time on her thigh. Her toes tingled as his hand reached all the way to her sensitive spot. Ebony looked around at the crowd uneasy. Could anyone else tell what was happening under their table cloth? She took a sip of wine turning towards him like they were having a conversation. Her mouth opened slightly as his finger rub in between her lips. Her butt shifted in the seat getting stuck to the leather.

"Stop it." She whispered in his ear while still focusing on the other patrons. His finger got deeper making her wetter. She bit her bottom lip wishing they were not in public. His finger moved quicker causing her fingers to twitch along with the rest of her body. Jefferson laughed at her.

"Check please." She asked the server.

....

Carson opened his eyes unaware of what time of day it was. The blinds were drawn and he couldn't see any sign of light coming through the cracks. He had called out from work two, maybe three days this week. It was all a blur. He looked at his cell phone that had several missed calls from India and Michael and an emotion less text from his wife. He threw his phone down on the side of the bed where his wife used to lay. Rubbing the empty side of the bed only reassured him that the separation was real.

Where did it all go wrong? From the moment he stepped out of the mover's truck and first laid eyes on his neighbor, Ebony had been it for him, and now she was gone, he had cheated on her, she had cheated on him and her sister was the only one he could connect to right now. This was not him at all. He was a good guy, not the guy he had become.

Banging came from the front door. Carson rolled over putting the pillow over his head hoping whom ever it was would go away. The banging got louder through the cotton. Carson threw the pillow across the room screaming. He stomped down the steps yanking the front door open.

"You're alive." His best friend looked him up and down in his red boxers and white undershirt. Carson left him standing at the door to return back to his bed.

"Dude, eww," Michael covered his nose as he walked into the bedroom, "It smells like funk and rotten eggs in here. When's the last time you took a shower?"

Carson climbed under the covers. "What day is it?"

"Oh my gosh." Michael put his hands on his forehead pacing the room.

"Wednesday. We are suppose to shoot some hoops remember?"

Michael stopped pacing starring at his best friend like he was pathetic. He threw an empty pizza box on the floor.

"This is not you, Mr. clean living in filth literally." Carson eyed his insensitive friend.

"My wife just left me. For once could you have some compassion?" Carson rolled out of the bed going into the bathroom.

"Brush your teeth while you're in there." Michael yelled after him.

Carson slammed the door behind him not having to go to the bathroom but wanting to get away from his friend. He leaned against the bathroom counter starring at his self in the square mirror. Looking at his white shirt that had pizza sauce on the front and coffee colored under arm stains, he realized how pathetic he really did look. He lifted his arms smelling each armpit.

"Oh that's bad." He said to himself. Maybe Michael was right although he would never say that to him. He splashed some cold water over his crust filled face before returning to the bedroom. Michael had a trash bag in his hand and was picking up the empty food wrappers from the last few days.

"Carson, you know I love you man, that's why I can't see you like this." He put the trash bag down to sit on the edge of the bed. Carson leaned against the dresser folding his arms.

"You and Ebony are classic. All great relationships go through tough times, that doesn't mean it's over and if you want this, and then you work for it, that's all."

Carson knew he was right, but wasn't ready to get out of his pity party.

"Enjoy this time to work on yourself so when she comes back, the two of you will be even stronger together." Carson was waiting for his friend to say lets go to the strip club and forget about your wife, not be sentimental. He unfolded his arms pushing himself up from the dresser. Michael stood up and met his best friend half way before embracing him in a manly hug.

"Now can we play some ball?" Michael extended his arm towards the door. "Spend some time with the fella's?" He did a little shimmy. Carson broke a smile. He appreciated his friend at that moment. Spending the last three days in a dark room was not helping anything. He was sure his wife wasn't doing the same so why give her the satisfaction.

"Give me thirty minutes."

TWENTY-FIVE

*E*bony tapped on the window to the studio door. Joe waved her in. He took off his head phone turning all his attention to her.

"You look like shit." She saw her reflection in the mirror. Pieces of hair sticking out of a messy ponytail, a stained shirt half tucked into her yoga pants; not being at home was starting to get to her. Joe looked her up and down.

"Girl you look like shit." He pointed to the small couch in the back of the studio. She sat down, joined her on it.

"I thought a lot yesterday." Her knee bounced up and down. "I have wanted this for so long and the thought of losing my marriage and maybe my family is killing me."

She clinched her hands together tucking them between her knees. "But if they can't stand by me and support my dreams, well then that's on them because I'm not giving up on this."

Joe broke out into a huge smile. Tears filled her eyes trying to believe her own words. Of all the people in the world, she expected Carson to be on her side. After everything they had been through, he had always promised to be there for her and he should want her to be happy. Singing made her happy.

Joe extended his arm letting Ebony fall into his armpit. He rubbed her shoulder.

"I knew you were going to say that. I saw the fire in your eyes when we first met and I knew nothing would stop you." He said quietly like he was talking to a baby. She closed her eyes causing the tears to fall down her cheeks.

"You and my best friend are only ones who has faith in me right now." he pulled back looking her in her eyes as she opened them. He grabbed her chin.

"You better have faith in yourself. I can't do this without you." She smiled nodding her head.

Ebony left the studio jumping on the train back to the suburbs. She hadn't seen her mother since the hospital and wanted to check on her.

Ebony walked into the office where she had worked for so many years. Rubbing her hand across the desk she sat at dreaming of a better life and now that it was starring her in the face, she was unsure.

"Is my mom busy?" She asked Jessica, the young assistant she had left in charge when she quit.

"Her appointment just left. She has an hour."

Ebony knocked two times then let herself in. Her mother was standing by the window looking like her old self. She had on a tweed pants suit, half inch brown heels and her hair was swept up in a neat bun and she assumed her glasses were sitting on the edge of her nose. She never turned around when the door opened, she stay fixated out the window. Ebony approached the window leaning opposite of her mother. She looked through the vertical blinds at all the trees that surrounded the office building. This is why she didn't live in the city, never to see the reds, oranges, and yellows of the tree tops. It was so beautiful and one of the things her father loved. She smiled at her mom slightly when she made eye contact with her. Ebony reached her hand out. Her mother starred at it then turned her eyes down. Ebony dropped her hand as her heart sank. Her mother had never been affectionate to her so she didn't know why she expected anything different today, but she had to try. The two women stood in front of the window silent. Ebony thought of her father, almost positive that her mother was doing the same.

"I'm sorry for how I acted at the hospital." Ebony broke the silence. She walked to the couch taking a seat. Her mother followed.

"It was a hard night." Her mother's bottom lip quivered. She was not prepared to deal with her mother crying again.

Ebony looked at her mother who had pulled her glasses off. She rubbed her tired eyes. Death is something that is inevitable but you never are really prepared for it especially when it happens unexpectedly. It just didn't seem fair to loose her dad at this point in her life where her career was about to take off but she could use his support to deal with her marriage.

Ebony shifted in her seat. Her and her mother had never had that loving bond and the past few months was the most they had seen each other. She always felt that her mother was jealous of the loving relationship she had with her father. Ebony leaned into her mother resting her head on her mothers shoulder hoping not to be rejected. Her mother sat like a statue. Tears flowed from Ebony's eyes. Ebony's body trembled as she let out a hard cry over everything. She cried for the loss of her father, she cried for her sisters misguidance, for her mother's resistance, and for her leaving her marriage and being in love with two men.

The two women sat on the couch motionless until Jessica buzzed in saying her one o'clock appointment had arrived. Ebony lifted her tear soaked face from her mother's suit jacket. Her mother stood up taking her jacket off throwing it to the side. Her daughter felt like that's how her mother felt about her feelings.

She wished she could have told her mother everything that was going on in her life, lie on the couch and talk to her like one of her clients. Maybe if she had booked her mom for a session then she would have gotten more out of her. At least she had made the effort for what is was worth.

....

Carson rubbed his tired eyes trying to focus on his computer after another sleepless night. That was his first day back to work in two weeks. Most men would love to have a break from their wife, but the separation was killing him. India had been very persistent since she found out her sister had moved out. She wanted to come over all the time and continue their affair and even though the attraction was there, he couldn't bring himself to go there again. He needed to find a way to get his wife back and her party would be a perfect time to make a big gesture.

"You going out for lunch?" Mike peeked his head into the office.

"What?" Carson looked up confused.

"Where you at man?"

"I need to get my wife back and I need to figure out how." Mike stepped into his office walking towards his desk to have a seat.

"Maybe she just needs time. Why don't you give her that and in the mean time you enjoy yourself."

Carson rolled his eyes. "I'm not interested in getting my freak on with anyone but my wife."

"That didn't stop you before." Carson shot him a dirty look. "I'm just saying." Mike shrugged his shoulders and laughed.

"I swear I don't know why I talk to you sometimes." Carson banged on his desk three times in frustration.

"I need to see Leslie."

Mike whipped his head up quickly looking at his friend like he had lost his mind. "Why?"

"That's the first step to getting Ebony back. She thinks Leslie is messing with her and I'm not doing anything about it so if I can prove she is still in the mental hospital, then that would be a start."

"You sound crazy right now." Michael stood up and walked out of the office shaking his head. Carson grabbed his keys.

"Remember she cheated on you, twice." Mike's voice trailed off as Carson ran down the hall hoping no one noticed he was gone.

Carson drove an hour into New Jersey to the mental health facility that he heard she was at. He pulled up into the curved driveway to the brown brick building. He approached the receptionist desk wondering if Mike was right. Was this a crazy idea? This would bring back all those horrible memories from the past year which he tried to bury.

Just beyond the desk he saw several patients walking around in a daze. His heart beat quickened as the nurse pointed to the television room where he was told Leslie was. He scanned the room looking for that sexy, energetic woman with the amazing body that he knew, but didn't see her. He spotted a thin woman starring out of the window curled up in a ball. He approached her slowly recognizing the face.

"Leslie?" He spoke softly. She turned her head slowly to face him.

"Carson?" He smiled at the recognition. He wasn't quite sure what to expect on the drive over.

"What are you doing here in the crazy house?" She put her hands in the air shaking them and laughing at the same time. She stood up and hugged her old friend. He tensed up not returning the hug. Was she still in love with him?

"You don't have to worry. My treatment is working and I won't hurt you." She sat back down in the window. "I never wanted to hurt you, I wanted to hurt..." She swallowed", "Her, your wife." Her bottom lip trembled. Her anger towards Ebony was definitely still there.

"So how are you?" He changed the subject sitting across from her in the window seat.

"Good. The treatment is working. I still love you, but know that I can't have you." She looked down at her hands twirling her thumbs in a circle. "How are things with you?"

He didn't know how to answer that. He couldn't possibly tell her the truth.

"I'm fine." She looked past him at the clock on the wall.

"It's time for group. You can stay if you want to?" He really wasn't ready to get back in the car after only ten minutes so he joined them for group therapy. Carson sat in the back of the room watching the group of six people talk in a circle. Leslie talked about her regret of hurting her brother and Ebony and how she knew it was wrong and accepted what she had done. Carson watched in awe. He was really proud of her. After group the two of them when for a walk in the courtyard. They laughed for over an hour talking about college years and their friendship. Carson had reservations in his mind about coming but being away from all the people in his everyday life that were causing him stress and pain right now was definitely a breather.

"I'm glad I came." The two sat down in a patch of grass.

"Me too. I've wanted to apologize to you for some time now and this was a great surprise." She put her hand on top of his. "Our friendship meant so much to me, more then a relationship even though I think we had incredible sex." Carson smiled thinking back." But seriously, I had a lot of childhood issues to deal with and just wanted to be loved." Their eyes met and he could see the pain which he never saw before. The strong Leslie he knew that never seemed to let things bother her was now so vulnerable and it showed. He truly felt remorse for her and wondered for a split second what if he would have chosen her back in college instead of his wife. He definitely wouldn't be going through all the crazy stuff he was going through now. Leslie would have never cheated on him, although he thought Ebony would never either.

"I should get going." He stood up helping her up as well.

"Thank you for coming Carson. I really do appreciate it. No one really comes to see me." She held her head down. Carson took her hand as they walked back to the main building.

"Since we are being so honest, have you been stalking my wife?"

Leslie looked sideways with a guilty pleasure on her face. I may have made a few things happen." She laughed a little. "I am sorry, but then I'm not." Carson starred at her not knowing how to reply. "I still have more work to do."

"You could have killed Ebony in that car attack."

Leslie looked shocked. "All I did was sent a note and some flowers that's all."

He gave her a slight smile believing her and she returned a big one.

He drove slower then normal on the way back to New York. Stopping for lunch, he was in no rush to get back to his life. Ebony was right about Leslie but Carson knew she wasn't going to do any harm but she probably wouldn't see it that way. Hopefully the truth would be a start to repairing their marriage besides the whole trust issue which was very hard to repair and the whole that it left in his heart would be even harder to fix. And if she ever found out about India, there would be no turning back for the two of them.

TWENTY-SIX

———————— ⟜⟞⟝ ————————

*E*bony was wearing a hole in the hotel carpet. It was six fifteen and the show started at eight. Melody knew that she had been stressing over her single release party for Weeks now and today was not the day to be late. A knock came from the door just as she picked up her cell phone to call her best friend again. Ebony yanked the door open with her face twisted up.

"Where the hell have you been? You were about to get left."

Melody glided into the room. "I'm sorry; it takes time to look this good." Melody wore a white jump suit with a sparkling plunging neck line and a pair of 4 inch open toed boots.

"The car has been outside for thirty minutes. You were about to get left."

Ebony rolled her eyes as she watched her best friend check out her backside in the full length hotel mirror.

"I can't with you today. Let's go." She grabbed a small bag and a long garment bag that was hanging in the coat closet as they ran out the door. She needed to figure something out soon because hotel life is only fun for a few days. Moving back to her parent's house was the most logical thing but that would depend if her sister was still residing there. She didn't feel like being around her at this point.

It was a short twenty minute ride to the club. The parking lot was half full. What if nobody comes out to see her? This was her first official coming out party as a new artist and it meant the world to her.

Carson was the first person she saw as she entered the main room. He was laughing so hard that he was wiping his eyes. Ebony smiled enjoying seeing him so happy until she saw the root of his happiness. Her sister who she didn't even know was coming had her hand on Carson's knee as they laughed uncontrollably about something.

"I want in on the joke." Ebony approached the happy couple eyeing her sister's hand which she snatched back quickly. Her husband jumped up to congratulate his wife. He kissed her cheek. Ebony pulled back quickly.

"I didn't know you were coming?" She turned to her sister.

"I forgot until your husband sent me a message. I have to support my big sister." She gave a sly smile that pissed Ebony off. Ebony looked her up and down taking notice of her skimpy black skirt and low cut tank top showing way too much cleavage, typical of her new sister the stripper. Ebony rolled her eyes and continued on to the back of the club. Joe was waiting for her backstage in a small dressing room with her name on the door.

"I thought you were going to bail on me." He grinned as she walked into the room.

"I would never do that." She hung up her dress bag on a hook on the back of the door. Unzipping the bag, she pulled out a short black dress.

"You like?" She showed Joe.

"No." Ebony's mouth dropped open.

"I had something better sent over." He nodded his head in the opposite direction. Ebony saw an emerald green dress with a low neck line and a lace back. Green was not her color but the dress was stunning.

"You?"

Joe shrugged his shoulders and smiled. Ebony gave him a hug before shoving him out the door. Once she slipped on the dress she stood in the mirror admiring herself. She had to admit the green went well with her skin color. Ebony paced back in forth waving her hands in the air so not to wipe them on her dress. A knock came from the door and she knew what that meant. One last look in the mirror, she applied her lipstick with a shaky hand. She started mouthing the words of her song over and over like she was going to forget if she didn't. She heard Joe on the microphone introducing her. There was a roar of applause as she made her way to the stage. Every time she stepped on stage felt like the first time. She had done this several times before but this time was different. Her career was on the line before it started. In two hours social media would either approve of her or eat her alive.

"I want to thank everyone for coming out tonight. I truly appreciate it and hope you all like this song and if not, just say you do." She grinned uncomfortably until the crowd chuckled a little making her feel at ease a little. She spotted India's hand on her husband's knee just before she closed her eyes taking one last breath before bellowing out her first note. By the second verse she was in her groove, dancing around the stage, getting her energy from the vibe of the audience. This was her destiny, where she was supposed to be. All those years she had spent wasting time doing things she didn't love because of the thought of failing as a singer, but thanks to Jefferson, he had brought all this back to her.

The crowd exploded in a cheer as she finished the first song. Her heart smiled. The crowd chanted for more. She looked to Joe for approval. He laughed and shrugged his shoulders. Ebony turned to the young guy who was on the drums and whispered in his ear. He started a slow tap with a ping of the percussion every fourth beat. She returned to the mic circling both hands around it. She closed her eyes and sang the ballot her and Joe had laid down a few days earlier. She opened her eyes by the second line but the crowd said nothing. It was hard to see faces through the bright lights but the front two rows gave her blank stares. Maybe she should have stopped while she was ahead. Ebony sang on because she loved the song that she had written and was proud of it. If no one else approved then oh well. She held the last note like Whitney Houston had done in so many songs. She took one last breath and smiled at the silent crowd taking a small bow.

"Thank you." She spoke softly into the microphone. A slow clap came from the crowd, probably her husband. Then the rest of the club joined in. People started whistling and cheering. The whole club was on their feet. She could see a few women wiping their eyes.

Back in the dressing room, she sat looking at herself in the mirror surrounded by tiny light bulbs. A smile crossed her face and the tears moistened her cheeks.

"I will be fine. I am strong and can survive all of this and I made the right decision." Ebony gave herself a pep talk. She dried her face, kicked off her shoes, and began jumping up and down to get out the rest of her energy. She could feel all the stress from the last few months leaving her body. Her sister, her husband, her mother, and losing her father all didn't seem to matter in that moment. She was living in her joy and that's all that mattered.

"Knock, knock." Her best friend pushed open the door and continued rejoicing with her friend.

"You were incredible and that second song, that was heart breaking. My best friend is going to be bigger than Beyonce."

Ebony stopped jumping. "Ok now you are exaggerating."

"I'm not. You need to believe in yourself as much as everyone else does." Ebony grinned knowing her best friend was right. "Get dressed so you can meet all your fans."

Melody shut the door behind her. It opened right back up as her husband walked in. They hadn't been alone in a room since the fight so she wasn't sure how the conversation would go.

"You were great." he said.

"Thanks," She focused on the floor as she swept her leg across it.

"How have you been?"

"I'm good, tired of the hotel, but I'm good." Ebony glanced up at him briefly then back down at the floor. "Thanks for coming."

Carson stepped to her grabbing her hands. "You know I have your back no matter what happens between us. I love you and that will never change, either as your husband or as your friend."

Ebony looked at him through tear filled eyes. "I know."

A knock came from the door causing the couple to release each other.

"I have a delivery for Mrs. Brody." A young woman set a huge vase of flowers down and left the room.

"Wow, you have lots of admirers." Carson commented.

Ebony pulled the card and it was blank. Carson looked over her shoulder probably wanting to see if they were from another guy.

"That's strange." He said as Ebony flipped the card back and fourth in her hand.

"No, I bet its Leslie again messing with me. She just won't stop."

Carson took a step back.

"About that." He started. Ebony took a seat because the look on his face scared her.

"I went to see her and she is still in the facility."

Ebony's eyes grew big. "Why would you do that?"

"I did it for us." She laughed in his face. "I was trying to put your mind at ease so you could stop fixating on her and thinking she's after you."

Ebony crossed her hands and legs. She didn't want to hear any more from him.

"I'm sure she loved that."

Carson's lips got thin. "That's not fair Ebony. She is getting the help she needs. She sent the note and flowers but it was harmless. I was just trying to help you out that's all."

Her husband stormed out the door. Ebony grabbed one of the colorful flowers and threw it at the door. She threw on a classy white pants suit and some heels, brushed her hair in a neat pony tail and left the room to get a drink. She entered the main room of the club unnoticed walking straight to the bar to order a drink. At the bar a few people asked for an autograph and a few pictures with her. After the crowd dispersed, Ebony leaned against the bar looking out at the club. She spotted her husband and her sister in a small hallway by the bathrooms. Ebony walked slowly towards them trying not to draw attention. They were in each others space and looked very intense. India had Carson by the arm and he was talking wildly with his hands. Probably mad about the blow up they had just had. Ebony stopped walking to watch the two from afar. What was really going on? Her sister stepped into Carson rubbing her hand down his cheek. The two starred at each other. Ebony's jaw dropped as she watched her sister kiss the man she had shared vows with and he actually returned the kiss before pulling back a few seconds later. Carson stepped away from her disappearing into the bathroom. The air became thick. Ebony grabbed her chest trying to get air in. She pivoted returning to the bar for a refill and a shot of tequila.

What did she just witness? Carson and India, that is crazy. Ebony stumbled grabbing onto the edge of the wooden bar to steady herself. She blinked her eyes quickly not sure what she really just witnessed. Carson and India? That can't be real. She kept repeating their names together in her head. Would her sister betray her like that? Would he? She was desperate to find out what was going on.

Ebony stabilized her feet on the floor taking small steps toward her sister until Carson returned from the bathroom. She watched her sister grip her husband's arm pulling him into her body again. They seemed to be in a deep conversation. Carson planted a kiss on her forehead then backed away. All the blood in her body rose to her head and threw her finger tips. She made a fist as she stomped through the crowd toward her sister forgetting her surroundings.

"You bitch." Ebony took her right fist making contact across her sister's face. High pitch screams came from the females close to them. Ebony grabbed a chunk of her sister's natural hair throwing her to the ground. India landed one good punch across Ebony's face as she straddled her sister, scratching her with her new fake nails. Ebony hated India's new trashy look but since she was a stripper now, it was only fitting. Ebony felt a pair of big hands grab her waist lifting her off the ground. She saw Joe out of her peripheral. Carson reached down helping India off the ground. He had some nerve.

"Stop this right now." Joe whispered in her ear. Her body went limp as she stopped fighting. She looked around at all the eyes starring at her. She felt her face burning and her career slip away from her.

Ebony paced the gravel parking lot after Joe had removed her from the club. She squinted as lights flashed in her face. Joe tried to shield her from the cameras until the car pulled up. He pushed her into the black sedan before it sped off.

"Can you circle around the block a few times then pull around back? I need to get my things.

Her purse was in the dressing room along with her best friend that she had left in the club and she was sure Melody was blowing up her cell phone right now. The car circled twenty minutes letting the paparazzi die down some before returning to the delivery entrance of the club. Ebony sat in the back seat bent over with her head in between her legs. What had she done? Starting a fight on her big night, this was not her at all.

"UUggh." She let out a grunt.

"You okay ma'am?" The driver looked back in the rear view mirror.

No, she wasn't all right. Her husband and sister were having some type of affair in front of her face. India had gotten out of control and this was unforgivable, even if she and Carson were separated, that's a line you don't cross.

Melody was waiting outside carrying all her friends stuff. Ebony smiled knowing there was one person she could always count on.

"What the hell happened?" Melody slid into the back seat handing Ebony her purse. She pulled out her cell phone seeing five missed calls from her so called husband.

"I saw my sister kiss Carson and there was clearly something going on between them."

Melody's jaw dropped. "What did he say because I know you confronted him?"

"That's where the fight came in. I just lost it and punched her before they could say anything." Ebony leaned back in the seat closing her eyes.

"Of all the people, I can't believe Carson would do something like this and with your sister of all people." Melody babbled on.

She was so right though. That was something she would expect from her best friend, it would hurt, but make more sense from her promiscuous best friend.

"Remember in junior high, India use to hang out whenever we had boyfriends over? I swear she would have slept with Bobby if she had the chance."

"Correction", Ebony sat up, "You had boyfriends over my house."

"But you liked Bobby and boy did she flirt with him with her young ass."

"You're not helping." Ebony leaned back. She looked at her best friend and busted out laughing; the best medicine right now.

....

"Fuck me now and hard."

Ebony stood in Jefferson's doorway surprised at herself. She was so angry at the happenings of the evening that he was the only person to make the pain go away temporarily. She had dropped her friend off then asked her driver to take her over to his house. She didn't want to show up to the hotel in fear of more reporters and she definitely didn't want to be alone.

"Is that a question or a demand?" Ebony rolled her eyes at him as she pushed past him letting herself in to the townhouse. It never occurred to her that he might have other female company after their last conversation about dropping by unannounced.

His lips were tight, teeth clenched, "I told you..." Jefferson started.

"I don't care what you told me, I said take me now."

Ebony surprised herself by the words coming out her mouth. It must have been the alcohol talking. She unhooked her dress letting it fall to the floor leaving her in heels and a black lace thong. The front door slammed shut. Jefferson walked towards her slowly. His hand ran up her bare chest grabbing her by the back of the neck. He yanked her close to his lips.

"Is this what you want? You want to be treated like the whore that you are." He pulled her by the neck, leading her into the living room. Flinging her body onto the couch, Jefferson unbuckled his jeans. They fell to the floor exposing his excitement. He took a handful of her hair pulling her to her feet, flipping her around; ass in air. She held her breath, bracing herself by holding onto the back of the couch. Ebony felt him enter from the back.

"Oh God." She let out a scream. Jefferson pounded out all the pain and anger she had felt towards her sister and husband, all the joy she had singing on the stage, and all the confusion that was still to come when she decided to face the people in her life and her new found fans. Her back side burned from his hands beating on her. His hands gripped her waist as he made one last thrust before convulsing. The couch caught her fall as her legs gave in. She kicked off her high heels; brought her knees into her chest and the tears moistened his couch. Jefferson sat beside her stroking her hair.

"You ready to talk because I don't know who that was that walked through my door? I liked it but that wasn't you."

She wiped her nose against her knee. "Tonight was my big night and I ruined it." She caught her breath between tears. "I saw my sister and Carson. I think they are having an affair."

Jefferson bust out laughing in her face. Ebony looked on with a straight face.

"Shit, you're serious. Not the boy scout."

"Do you have to be an ass?"

"That's what you like."

"But not when I need you right now." Ebony stood up gathering her dress off the ground. Jefferson came after her. He grabbed her from behind, squeezing her waist tightly forcing the tears to come back out of her eyes. He held her for what seemed to be an eternity as she lost all composure of herself. He was not the most compassionate man, but at this point all she wanted was a pair of strong hands to hold her and make her feel like everything would be all right.

TWENTY-SEVEN

―――――― ⤜⤚ ――――――

The house he once shared with his wife that he use to love coming home to now seemed like a strange, empty place. Carson sat in the darkness of his kitchen with the street light flickering through the window. He twirled the small shot glass on the table barely able to see the dark liquid in it. Why did he let India get that close to him at the bar and why did he kiss her on the forehead? This was his fault and he had no idea how to make it right.

A light knock came from the front door. He didn't move from the breakfast bar. There is no one in the world he wanted to see right now except his wife and he knew it wasn't her. What had he done? There was no turning back from this now. He had gotten caught and even though she cheated first, this was the ultimate betrayal and it may have cost him the love of his life. He emptied the glass before filling it back up again. A gush of light came through the house as the front door flew open. Damn it, she would have a key. His blurry eyes saw his biggest mistake standing in front of him.

"I didn't answer the door for a reason."

"I wanted to check on you." India walked slowly towards him. "You left the club in such a hurry." Her hand brushed the top of his.

"Don't." He snatched his hand back. "You caused this." He took the liquid in the glass back and filled it up again. India grabbed the bottle out of his hand.

"I didn't force your dick in me now did I? I won't let you blame me for all of this. We did this together."

Carson snatched the bottle back knowing she was right. He had a moment of weakness or two that he wished he could erase. India leaned over the bar, her breath tickling his nose hairs, "I didn't want her to find out this way either, but it happened so now we must deal with it." Her hand rubbed down his cheek. For a moment he saw the old India, the one full of compassion who loved her sister, not the back stabbing one she had become. Carson's eyes burned with tears. He closed them allowing the droplets to roll down his cheeks collecting in the palm of her hand.

"I need to be alone." he sniffed, removing his face from her embrace. "Leave."

India starred at him, eyes wide. She must have been surprised by his words. He wanted to be comforted, but not by her. India walked slowly to the front door shutting it behind her. Carson locked the door, slinking down against it. He cried like a baby. How would he make this better? How could he get his wife back? What was she up to at that moment? He knew she had questions and he wanted to explain everything to her but he was probably the last person she would talk to, so he would have to go to the next best person.

....

Ebony climbed into the bed curling her body up in a ball. She wanted to be in her own bed at her house, but that was not an option. She fluffed up a pillow behind her and then grabbed another one holding it tightly. Not knowing the truth was killing her. What was really going on? She needed answers but wasn't ready to face Carson or her sister. Did anyone else know about this? Melody? Her mom? Ebony closed her eyes trying to drift off to sleep and end this nightmare of a day. She flicked on the television after starring at the ceiling for twenty minutes. The news flashed the video of her being ushered out of the club, the late show made several jokes about her as well. She flicked the channel to something lighter. BET was playing a Tyler Perry movie which seemed safe for her to watch. Was this really what she wanted? People in her business and her life at all times just because she wants to make people happy with her voice. Maybe the best thing to do is distance herself from her family and focus on her music and she would not have to sneak around with Jefferson anymore. They could make it official.

....

The sun crept through the small opening in the curtains. Ebony yanked them open letting the light flood into the room. She inhaled deeply then exhaled slowly, smiling at the beautiful day ahead of her, hoping that the world had moved on from her little mishap last night. It was a new day and she planned on taking back her life. What good would it do to wallow in the mistakes of the past? If Carson wanted her sister then more power to the both of them. She had an incredibly sexy man that knew how to put it down. Although he could be an ass, the good out weighed the bad.

Her cell phone buzzed on the night stand. Joe sent her a text wanting to meet up today at 4pm. She hit up Melody to see if she were free today. It was time to get out of the hotel room. She didn't want to consider the option of moving back to her childhood home anymore. India was the last person she wanted to see. After a quick shower, she threw on a warm up suit from BeBe, a pair of sunglasses, and a loose pony tail as she headed down to breakfast. She sat at a two seated table in the corner of the hotel restaurant keeping her sunglasses on. The server brought her a glass of water and orange juice.

"Aren't you Ebony Lovely?" Her maiden name sounded better as a stage name.

"Yes." She said quietly not ready to defend herself against critics.

The server smiled. "I love your song. I can't wait for your album. Can I get your autograph?" The server handed her a small pad she was writing orders down on. Ebony signed it before ordering a cheese omelet and a bowl of fresh fruit.

"Morning hussy." Melody flopped in the chair opposite her. "How are you this morning?"

"I'm good." She gave a genuine smile. Melody twisted her face looking confused.

"Really? It's time for me to get my life back together; find my own place, try to fix the mess I caused last night. I will deal with Carson and India later. I can't be worried about them right now."

"I'm glad you are positive this morning." The server dropped off her breakfast.

"Do you want something?"

"No I'm good." Melody picked up the extra set of silverware and took a bite of her friend's eggs.

"I thought you were good?"

"I am." She said with a mouth full.

Ebony laughed at her best friend. She was happy to have her here right now even if she was going to eat all her breakfast.

"You know", Melody swallowed, "Carson asked if we could meet up today. He wants to talk to me probably about you."

"Are you going to meet him?" Ebony took a sip from her orange juice.

"Do you want me to?"

She lowered her glass slowly trying to swallow the juice in her mouth. Melody could be a mediator between the two of them; she just never thought he would reach out to her so soon. Was she really ready to know what was going on? Just when she was focused on not focusing on their drama, it was all about to come to light by the end of the day.

She swallowed. "Sure you can meet him if you want. I can't tell you what to do." She should have known her husband would pull the best friend card but it didn't really matter what he had to say. What excuse could he possibly give?

The ladies finished breakfast then headed off into the city. They saw a few studio and one bedroom apartments that were way over priced for the little bit of space they gave, but that was New York. They also took a short train ride outside the city and saw a few apartments for a better price and more space. It was almost three by the time they had seen about ten places. The ladies headed back to the city. Even though it wasn't worth it, Ebony really wanted to be in the city. She could walk everywhere and she would be closer to the studio.

"I've been so wrapped up in my own shit; I haven't even asked how things have been with you. I'm a terrible friend." Ebony said as the walked down the block.

Melody sighed then smiled slightly. Ebony knew she was about to drop a bomb.

"Well," She started slowly, "Keith did apologize and wants to make things work."

Ebony stopped on the crowded street getting bumped by the bustling work crowd trying to get back from lunch.

"And I know you didn't fall for that. If he hit you once this early on, he's bound to do it again."

"I know, I know." She said reluctantly. They started walking again slowly. "But you slept with him didn't you?"

"It was just some goodbye sex. He just doesn't know it yet." Melody laughed.

"That's not funny." Ebony gave her the serious face. Melody always takes sex so casual but its different when papers are involved and when he crossed that line he should never get any EVER again.

Ebony pointed her finger at her best friend, "You better not go back to him or I'm done with you."

Melody stopped in her tracks with her mouth wide open and her eyes to match.

"Wow bitch that's harsh."

"I'm serious. All I need is to hear I lost my best friend to some stupid domestic abuse. I'm not having that."

Melody knew she was serious. Ebony loved people in her inner circle hard and she couldn't lose someone else close to her, her father was enough.

"Why don't we look at two bedrooms?" Melody suggested as she flipped through an apartment guide needed to change the subject.

"Look, here's one in the meat packing district. This looks nice and it's not that expensive."

Ebony grabbed the book from her liking what she saw. She looked at her cell phone.

"We have a few minutes. Want to check it out?"

"Yes." She smiled at her friend never thinking that they both needed a permanent place to stay and how fun it would be for them to be roommates. Just like college except without all the men coming in and out and the parties. Who was she kidding, Melody never changes but hopefully she won't be home a lot.

"Let's meet up tonight because I want to know what my sorry ass husband has to say." Ebony hugged her best friend as they parted. She was off to meet Joe and Melody to meet Carson. They had put in an application on the two bedroom apartment telling the leasing office that they needed to move in ASAP so hopefully they would hear something back in a few days. The thought of returning to the house to get her things made her sick to her stomach.

Joe hit her up to meet at a coffee shop instead of the studio. That didn't seem like a good sign. What if they were dropping her before she even got started? Could they void her contract? She should have read it closer. Maybe she would have to move back with her mom and start all over again.

Joe was the first person she noticed as she opened the door to the shop. There were only three other people in there getting carry out coffee probably trying to finish the rest of their work day. Joe was not alone. A beautiful exotic woman with long black hair was with him. She looked slightly familiar but Ebony couldn't place her face. She hugged Joe before taking a seat.

"This is Robyn Ashby. She is going to be your best friend over the next few weeks." Ebony smiled at her to be polite but the woman was focused on her cell phone texting intensely. "So the other day was great, then a mess and now it's clean up time and she is the clean up woman."

Joe folded his arms leaning back against the chair with a huge smile on his face like he had just discovered the cure for cancer or something.

Ebony stood back up, walked to the counter to order a coffee which she hardly ever drank, and then returned to her seat. Joe starred at her puzzled.

"Are you ok? I'm sorry I should have started off like that. I can't imagine how your feeling."

"I'm good." She took a sip from her coffee as her eye twitched. The third party at the table finally looked up from her phone.

"Sorry, I had to get those last two dates booked." Robyn extended her hand across the table along with a beautiful smile.

"So what is actually going on?"

"So," She flipped her long hair from one side to the other, "We are going to make the media love you and forget all about that little incident the other day. I have booked a few appearances on morning shows, talk shows stuff like that and a few appearances at children's hospitals and a homeless shelter. Are you good with that?"

Ebony took another long sip from her cup. Honestly all she could think about was what Melody and her husband were talking about at that moment.

"I'm good with that." Her reputation was on the line and she needed to do anything to fix it. Ebony knew she was a likeable person but the media would have her looking like some young ratchet person who can't control their attitude.

"We leave tonight for a late show appearance then go from there. We will be on the road for about a week." Robyn explained.

"And we will be promoting the single at the same time. A few of those appearances you will be performing also. Robyn will coach you on answering questions about the fight. You will be fine."

Ebony left to go pack a bag and check out of the hotel. There was no need to spend extra money. She could stay with her mom or best friend for a few days when she got back. Hopefully the apartment will have come through by then. She tried to call Melody to cancel dinner for tonight but she didn't answer. She could only imagine what kind of nonsense he was feeding her.

TWENTY-EIGHT

*C*arson sat in the bar lobby starring at his second drink. The bar had beautiful rosewood walls with large chandeliers hanging everywhere. Mike had told him about this place. He couldn't meet her at the strip club so he chose a classy place he had never been to. Carson looked at his watch. Late as always. He tapped his fingers against the bar. Melody was like a sister to him so why was he so nervous. Melody had a strong personality and he needed her to believe him so she would tell Ebony how sorry he was.

Maybe she changed her mind about coming. Maybe this was a bad idea. Maybe he should have went to Ebony directly and made her listen to him, involving a middle man may not have been the best decision.

"Fancy spot. I like this." Melody gave him a quick hug before taking the empty stool next to him. She seemed to be in a good mood.

"So what's up and where's my drink? Don't act brand new." Carson lifted his hand to signal the bartender.

"You know what I want." Carson jumped right in. "Your girl won't answer my calls and I need to explain what happened.

Melody rubbed her forehead. "How do you explain sleeping with her sister?" Melody had no filter. "Some random bitch, ok, but her sister?"

Carson could feel his face getting red. "She slept with Jefferson. Nobody seems to care that she carried on this affair for months and probably going on again now."

He apparently had no filter today either or it was the alcohol. He wanted to swallow the words right after they came out but it was too late.

"I know there is no excuse but I am sorry and I need her to know that." He hung his head and finished his drink. "Our marriage has been a mess but I love her dearly and can't lose her."

"How do you expect her to accept the two of you?" Melody gave her a disgusted look.

"I was drunk which is no excuse. You know she's been working at the strip club and we've been spending time there because she is never home and we started flirting. Then you two went out of town and she made me dinner because I was lonely and..."

Melody put her hand up. "Ok, I don't want to know any more. They both took a long slow sip from their drinks. "We've been back a few weeks now. So you hid this all this time?"

"Was I supposed to publicize it? I just need to know how to fix this." Carson motioned for another refill.

"Well drinking yourself into a coma won't fix it and frankly it's going to take time. That's her sister. Those two will have to repair their relationship before you two do. I wish I had an answer but it's just going to take time and she may never recover from this."

"Her words fell on him like a pile of bricks. Had he really lost her forever? Maybe she had already told Melody that she was done with the marriage and she was sparing his feelings right now, or maybe he had given her an out to go pursue something with Jefferson. He had so many questions that can only be answered by one person.

"Well then, I guess there's nothing left to say." Melody touched the top of his hand. I will see her tonight and talk to her. I don't want to see the two of you like this; I'm just a realist that's all."

Carson placed his hand on top of hers and gave her a half smile. Melody gave him a hug and a kiss on the cheek before leaving him alone. He caught his reflection in the mirror on the wall. What to do now? Go home to an empty house? Go to the strip club and run into India or sit here drowning his sorrows when all he wanted to do was curl up with the woman he loved and make love to her all night. Carson ordered a few more drinks. His head got heavy leaning on the bar.

"You alright man?" The bartender asked after drink number six. "Can I call someone for you?"

Carson's eyes met his through blurry vision. He picked up his phone which was lying on the bar and laughed.

"No one loves me. There's no one to call." The bartender took his phone and dialed the last number on the phone. Thirty minutes later his sister in law walked through the door.

....

Carson rolled up in a ball grabbing his head. The pounding was so loud. He reached to the night stand grabbing a bottle of aspirin. This was not the first hangover he's had over the last several weeks so that bottle had come in handy many mornings. He swallowed two pills then leaned back into his pillows. He rubbed his eyes trying to focus them. Looking across the bed to see his wife's alarm clock, he noticed a slim naked body sleeping next to him. Carson pulled back starring at the sleeping woman. He smacked his forehead turning his back to the woman.

"What did I do?" The woman moaned stretching her arm around his waist grabbing him. She kissed his shoulder. "Good morning." India spoke in his ear as she nibbled on it at the same time.

"What are you doing in my bed?" He grabbed the blanket pulling it close to him to cover his bare chest.

"You're welcome for getting you home safely."

"What?" He slunk down into the bed covering his head with the blanket. He remembered drinking at the bar after he talked to Melody but nothing else came to mind. Did he really sleep with her again? This is number 3 or 4? He was losing count. This had to stop. It was very good and he loved it, but it was forbidden. It's his wife's sister. Carson rolled out the bed to put his boxers on. His dick was soft which is usually strange for a guy waking up so maybe they did have sex. One time he could justify, but this many times he couldn't justify to his wife.

"I need coffee and you need to leave." He never turned to face her. He didn't want to look at her let alone his self in the mirror.

"I can take you to get your car."

"I'll find a way." He snapped. He would just call Mike since these days he resembled his nasty best friend.

Carson threw on a t-shirt and walked into the kitchen. Turning the coffee pot on, he grabbed the first mug from the cupboard. He looked at it and saw his wife's face. She had given him that mug back when they were dating. It was the first night they had spent together. Ebony had made him a cup of coffee after an incredible night of making love. She had placed the black mug with a big red heart on it and his name on the back in front of him. Her beautiful smile lit up the room and his heart. He knew at that moment that she was to be his forever.

"AAHH" The cup went flying across the kitchen crashing on the wall into little pieces.

"What the hell." India ducked trying not to get hit by flying pieces.

"Get out." He shouted. India looked at him like he were a stranger. That's what he felt like these days. He didn't even know himself. The drinking, the outbursts, and wild sex acts were not him at all. India left without saying another word. Maybe she would finally get the hint. The less he saw of her the better. He could not sleep with her anymore. The person he had become over the last couple weeks did not agree with him. Missing work, being drunk, that was so out of his character and it couldn't continue. It was time to get his life back with or without Ebony.

TWENTY-NINE

*E*verything happened so fast. Ebony took her seat in first class with Robyn. It didn't make sense to her to start her promotional tour in L.A when New York has so much to offer; The Today show, Wendy Williams, she could have started anywhere else.

"I hope we can go sight seeing." Ebony grinned at Robyn who didn't look amused.

Ebony took her cell phone out to turn it off. She still hadn't heard back from her best friend hoping she had received her message and didn't think she stood her up for dinner. Ebony was dying to know what her husband had to say. Carson had already left several I'm sorry messages but none of them seemed to matter. She felt like Carrie from Sex in the City when Mr. Big had broken her heart, but she couldn't throw her cell phone in the ocean. She was trending now and needed to stay abreast of what people were saying about her, especially after her episode at the club the other night.

Six hours later, the town car was driving through Hollywood with the warm night air hitting her face. She felt like a little kid. It was her first trip to the west coast and so far it was just like what you see on television. Beautiful people walking or pushing their little dressed up dogs down the street and it was like summer time all the time. She may have to trade in her busy streets of New York for all this one day. It would definitely be a fresh start away from everyone.

"We have a tight schedule." Robyn said coldly. Ebony was starting not to like her very much.

By the time she climbed into the bed at the Ritz Carlton, she had already made an appearance on the late late show and a small night club. The three hour time difference was throwing her off. She let out a big yawn as she checked her cell phone. Melody had finally returned her message saying their conversation went well but she didn't want to bother her with the details and they would catch up when she got back into town.

Ebony relaxed into the feather pillows. She inhaled deeply then let it out slowly.

Finally everything was coming together. Maybe it was time to let her marriage go. There really was no forgiving Carson and India especially in the near future. She and Jefferson could be together finally without sneaking around. This was what she wanted. After all he was the reason why she had a career right now.

She left a message for Jefferson saying she needed to talk to him when she got back. This was a new chapter in her life. Carson was part of the old one and she needed to put all that behind her. She wished India could go in that chapter too but unfortunately she was blood and would be around forever.

....

A week later, Ebony's plane touched down in New York. Home sweet home. Ebony hailed a cab. Leaving the airport, she remembered that she had checked out of the hotel and didn't have anywhere to go. She threw her suitcase in the back seat wondering how her whole life fit into it. The promotion tour continued tomorrow morning and right now she just wanted a nice meal and good night sleep. She felt like she could sleep for twenty-four hours especially with the three hour time change from L.A.

The cab driver dropped her off at her childhood home. Ebony starred at the brick structure not wanting to go in but having no where else to go.

"Hello," she called out. The house seemed empty. Her mother should have been at work anyway. Using her key, she let herself in dropping her suitcase by the front door. She walked into the kitchen to raid the refrigerator. There was a half eaten pizza, some lunch meat, yogurt, and a couple cartons of juice.

"I should have stopped somewhere to get something to eat." Her car was still parked by the hotel so she would have to get that later on, but first she needed sleep. Ebony had a glass of water then closed the fridge.

"What the hell?" India was standing on the other side of the door starring at her.

"Why are you here?" India asked.

"None of your business." Ebony moved to the side and her sister moved with her not getting out of her way. Was this really going to happen right now? She was too tired to kick her sister's ass right now.

"You don't live here."

Ebony laughed uneasily. "I can't do this with you right now." She took one hand pushing her sister to the side.

"Don't touch me." India was very defensive for some reason. Ebony should be the one pissed not India. She had no right to have an attitude. India pushed her sister in the back causing her to stumble. Ebony whipped around with balled fists.

"You want to fight? Bring it on bitch." India yelled at her.

"What is your problem? You slept with my husband. You have no reason to have an attitude." Ebony thought her anger had subsided until she saw her sister again and it all came back. She shouldn't be talking to her right now; they should be wrestling on the floor.

"You," India put her finger in her sister's face, "Are a spoiled brat. You don't deserve Carson. I have always liked him and you took him away from me." Ebony's mouth dropped. "And now dad is gone, you have no one to be on your side and you hate that. Well good. It's about time you are the outsider of this family like I have been for so long but wait now your going to be a famous superstar so yet again I lose."

Ebony took a few steps back grabbing the kitchen counter next to her. She had never heard her sister talk to her like that and she had no remorse for sleeping with her husband.

"This is not a competition. This is my life. Carson and I have been together forever. You never went after him and you act like it was ok to sleep with him which it's not and don't be mad about the decisions I have made in my life. You chose to shake your ass on a pole. I have a gift and I am pursuing it and don't talk about our father cause I will smack the shit out of you."

Ebony started pacing the small kitchen. Her blood was boiling and she felt another fight coming on. She looked at her sister sideways. They had never been extremely close, but the way India was acting was beyond absurd.

"You have Jefferson now, so let Carson go to be with me."

Ebony's eyes grew big. "Who are you?" Is all she could manage to say? Her blood was boiling inside. She shook her head as she walked off to grab her suitcase and find another place to rest her head. The way she felt, she thought she could really hurt her sister at this moment. She called a cab and waited outside. She couldn't stand to be around her sister for one more minute.

"What's wrong now?" Jefferson flung the door open allowing Ebony to walk in. She had left her mom's, got her car, and text Jefferson to see if she could stop by. Ebony yawned as she pulled up to his town house. All she wanted to do was sleep before she had to make another appearance tonight. Her sister had managed to stress her out again. Someway, somehow she would have to separate herself from all this drama and put her life together. Hoping this would be a start as she wanted to talk to Jefferson about the two of them. Joe had given her the name of a lawyer to draw up divorce papers. As much as she loved her husband, there was no coming back from all of this.

"I don't have a place to stay because I checked out of my hotel, my sister is at my mom's house and I can't be around her, and I can't go home so I'm here." She shrugged her shoulders feeling completely alone.

"Are you asking to stay here?" She patted his chest so he could let out the breath he was holding in.

"No I'm not. You're safe. I do want to talk to you about something."

"Yeah I got that text. What's up?"

They walked to his couch to take a seat. He starred at her intently which was strange because he usually didn't give his undivided attention.

"So I'm going to file separation papers. I don't think I can get over what he's done."

Jefferson leaned back into the cushions. "Well that's good. You don't need that anyway. You need to focus on your career."

"What if I want more?" Ebony stood up in front of him. She unbuttoned her jeans and lifted her t-shirt over her head standing in only a light pink bra set. A slight smile came across his face. Straddling his legs on the couch, Ebony put her lips to his.

"So this is why you came over here?" He said softly.

"You never disappoint me." Stroking his already big ego, but it was truth. The sex with him was incredible and she enjoyed every time, even the rough ones. Her hands unbuttoned his pants as she licked her lips. His hands unsnapped her bra, tossing it to the carpet. He encompassed her face kissing her one more time. His finger tips dragged down her shoulders stopping at her breasts. His fingers twirled her hard nipples causing her to giggle. Ebony arched her back leaning her head backwards taking in the incredible feeling. His hands moved to her spine as his tongue circled her right nipple before engulfing her whole breast.

"Oh God." She cried out snapping her head back up. Jefferson stopped locking eyes with hers. She felt the connection. She knew the feelings for him were real. Over the past year she had been infatuated with this man, hated him, and now have grown to love him. But could she tell him that? He would run in the opposite direction. He had not expressed a desire to be involved and everything she knew about him told her that he didn't want to be settled, but they had been very physical and she didn't want to believe that he was sleeping with someone else as well.

Ebony stood up pulling his pants off. She wet her lips and tasted all of his goodness. His hands slid in her hair caressing her scalp, guiding her at the same time. His moans made her smile inside. When his leg started to tremble she stood up basking in the beauty of his fulfillness. He grabbed her waist guiding her on top of him. The two danced in a rhythmic motion, nice and slow. Every now and then he would stop moving and move her waist pushing her body down for him to go deeper inside. She grabbed his shoulders as the pleasurable pain intensified. His hand cupped her butt before landing a hard smack across her right cheek. She bounced quicker. Jefferson bit his bottom lip and she knew it was all over. She laughed at the fact that she knew his sexual faces.

Ebony sat on the couch next to Jefferson, hand lingering on his knee. She looked at his post sex face glistening with little sweat droplets.

"Can I ask you something?"

His face dropped probably feeling the serious tone in her voice. He shook his head.

Ebony slid to the edge of the couch. "How do you feel about me being separated?"

"I told you I think it's good." He stands to his feet walking to the kitchen. Ebony watches his fine physique as he drinks a beer from the fridge. She gets up following him.

"But what about us? When I am a free woman, what will happen?"

"If you're trying to say something, just say it. I don't read signs."

Ebony crossed her arms not liking the tone coming from him.

"I think we should see where this is going?" She reached out touching his arm. He pulled it back slightly. Ebony's eyes widened as she took a step back.

"I think you need to focus on your career and getting your life together. We hook up, have amazing sex but I'm not looking for anything else. I thought that was understood."

Ebony walked back towards the couch grabbing her scattered clothes. She got dressed in a hurry and ran out the door without looking back at Jefferson or speaking another word to him. She slammed her car door just as the tears started to fall. She saw Jefferson open the front door but it was in her rear view mirror.

THIRTY

C arson taped up the third box of his wife's things in the bedroom. It had been two months now since they had spoken or seen each other. He was back to his normal schedule of the gym and work and had not spent any time with anyone from that family. Against his better judgment he had listened to his boy Mike and let Ebony have her space after his talk with Melody. He had thought that his confession would bring her to him to talk, but she had stayed away so he did as well despite how much it hurt.

The door bell rang snapping him out of his depression. Mike stood there with an unusual look on his face, not his usual cocky smile. It was Wednesday and he had offered to pick up Carson for basketball which was awfully kind for him.

"You look like I feel inside." Carson said pulling the front door wide open.

"That dirty skank from the club got me burning."

Carson backed up.

"Don't do me like that." Mike stepped into the house.

"Maybe I should drive myself because I know you had sex in the car." Carson chuckled until a professional looking white man appeared behind Mike.

"Are you Carson Brody?" He asked. Mike turned around in defense mode.

"Who wants to know?" He spoke for his best friend whose throat had suddenly become dry.

"You have been served." The guy leaned past Mike handing Carson a manila envelope. Carson took it then let it slip from his finger tips as he stepped back sitting on the steps. He didn't have to open the envelope to know what was inside. Was Ebony really doing this? After everything they had been through, this really couldn't be the end. He had to talk to her. Enough was enough. This woman meant the world to him and his heart wasn't ready to say goodbye.

"I think I'm going to pass tonight." Carson picked up the envelope off the floor. Mike snatched it from his grasp.

"No your not. I'm not going to let you sit here and stare at some divorce papers all night, be sad, and drown your sorrows in a beer or worse." Carson looked up at his friend through his burning eyes. Michael's face softened as he bend down to Carson's level.

"I'm really sorry that you are going through this. You and Ebony have always been great together, but like I said before, if it's meant to be then it will be."

He put his arm on his best friends shoulder. Carson stood up and hugged him.

"That's enough mushy stuff." Michael pushed him off. "Let's go."

Carson grabbed his bag following Mike out the door.

The gym was packed. This was the championship game before they took a three month break for the summer. Carson scanned the stands hoping that he would see a familiar face but after those papers, he knew better. They greeted the rest of their team before taking off their outside clothes exposing their gym clothes. Carson grabbed a loose basketball taking a few warm up shots. The ball hit the backboard rolling to the side lines. Carson followed the ball as it stopped at a pair of black tennis. He bent down grabbing the ball. Standing up, Jefferson was starring him in the face with a smug grin.

"Having some trouble focusing? I heard about your little situation." Jefferson's hand reached out landing on Carson's shoulder. His eyes grew big before yanking his shoulder out of the grasp of the man sleeping with his wife. The ball slipped from Carson's grip. His fist closed up with all the anger from his world ending. The future that he had planned out with his best friend, their kids, and all their dreams seemed to have ended because of the man in his face.

"We're about to start." Carson heard Mike say as his best friend rested his hand on his shoulder. Carson let out a huge breath as he unclenched his fist.

"I went to see your sister." Carson said between clinched teeth. "I think I was too quick to forgive you last year. She clearly has issues but you know better." Carson stepped in closed to Jefferson almost nose to nose. He felt Mike take a step closer as well in case someone threw a punch. "You have ruined my life. That's not something easily forgotten." Carson took a step back before turning around to walk away.

"If your marriage was solid, I wouldn't have been able to slide in there and that pussy… oh how it loves me." He spoke loud enough for Carson to hear. That was the Jefferson he knew; the asshole. Carson stopped. He could feel his face boiling. He lifted his head making eye contact with his best friend. Carson turned his head slowly eyeing Jefferson. This time he had gone too far. He had disrespected his wife in front of him. All the anger and hurt that had been weighing on his shoulders for the past few months showed all over his face. Before he could take a step to him, Mike had wiped the smirk off Jefferson's face for him. Jefferson fell to the ground in the middle of the court. The whole gym grew silent as Carson and Mike grabbed their belongings and left the gym.

THIRTY-ONE

SIX MONTHS LATER

*E*bony threw her bags down in the middle of the living room. Since her and Melody had moved into their apartment she had spent a total of about seven nights in the apartment. She flopped down on the couch kicking off her shoes. Ebony leaned back onto the couch closing her eyes. She had been all over the country for the last six months. At first she was hesitant when Joe had asked her to be the opening act for a big pop star but she realized that she needed to be away from her sister, Carson, Jefferson, and even her mother. She was only going to be home for two weeks before heading back out. Unfortunately she had to be in court in two days for her divorce. She let out a huge sigh not knowing if she was ready to see him. She definitely missed him but wasn't sure if she missed them.

Her eyes opened as she heard keys rattling in the door. Ebony looked around noticing the bright red couch she was sitting on, the bright yellow walls screaming from the kitchen and the tangerine walls behind her. She shook her head realizing that she should have never left her best friend alone to decorate the place. Melody walked in the door letting out a huge scream when she noticed Ebony sitting on the couch. The two embraced.

"I have missed you bitch. I'm so glad you are back. This place is lonely without you."

"Are you sure? These walls seem to be screaming at me."

"Ha-ha." Melody let go of her friend. "I want to hear all about your tour. I've been following you on social media. I can't believe I'm best friends with a superstar."

"Please. I am hardly a superstar." They sat back down on the couch. "I know I'm starving and all I want is some pizza."

"We can definitely do that." Melody hoped off the couch grabbing her cell phone to order a pizza.

"You didn't decorate my room did you?" Ebony asked standing from the couch.

"No bitch." Ebony grinned as she picked up her suitcases and carried them to her room. She couldn't wait to get a good night sleep in her own bed. Dinner was on its way, she wished she could call Jefferson to release her stress. He hadn't had any contact with her since she ran out of his house several months ago. Getting turned down by him had hurt her especially since she poured her heart out but deep down she knew that they wouldn't have worked out. That's who he was, a person who was self absorbed and did not want love in his life, just sex. Saying goodbye to him in her heart was bittersweet but for the best. Her mother was a different story. She had checked in on her mother once a week while she was gone but going to see her was a different story.

She heard a knock at the door as she unzipped her suitcase.

"I know the pizza is not here already." She yelled out into the living room.

"No it's not the pizza." Ebony froze. That was the last voice she had wanted to hear. She turned to see India standing in her doorway. Carson or her sister hadn't crossed her mind in months until her plane touched down at LaGuardia Airport.

"Hello." Her sister spoke.

"Hi."

Ebony turned back around to focus on her suitcase.

"Can we talk?"

"I can't stop you."

India came closer taking a seat on the edge of her bed. She didn't want her in her eyesight but now she couldn't ignore her sister. Being in her presence brought back all the issues that she had put in the back of her mind six months ago. Maybe she needed to move away from New York and put real distance between all the people she didn't want to face; her sister being number one on the list.

"Mom is doing much better. She is back to work." Ebony shook her head like she didn't really care but she already knew that. "I've done some soul searching over the last several months. I think it was me being a stripper and losing daddy that made me act out." Her hand crept closer to her sisters. Ebony yanked hers back before her sister could touch her.

"Don't use dad as an excuse."

"I'm not going to lie to you, I have always wanted Carson since he moved in next door to us all those years ago. But he took one look at you as kids and that was it, I never had a chance." India turned her back to her sister moving her arm up to her face. "So when the two of you started having problems, I just thought it was my chance. I knew it was wrong, but I just wanted some one to love me. Those guys at the club treat me like a piece of ass... I just wanted to be treated like a woman for once."

Ebony stood motionless. Hearing that from her own sister broke her heart but she still could have picked someone besides Carson, anyone else.

India sat on the edge of the bed hunched over. She sighed. "I was mad at you for having cheated on him and that all your dreams were coming true. I don't have a career or anything going for me so I was jealous. I know I was wrong." Her finger tips trembled knowing she was in arms length to reach out and grab her sister by the throat. Ebony could feel India's eyes on her even though she wouldn't make direct contact with her. Her sister's breath warmed her arm. India grabbed some dirty clothes out of the suitcase tossing them in the hamper to help her sister. Ebony knew what she was trying to do. She knew an apology was hard for her and she couldn't only be mad at her sister, her husband was just as much to blame. India nudged her sister in a playful manor. Ebony fell slightly to the side. Eyeing her sister sideways she paused. A slight smile broke on her face as she pushed her sister back lightly.

"Pizza's here." Melody yelled out from the other room.

"You want to stay for dinner?" India and Ebony's eyes met for the first time in months. Her eyes filled with water droplets. Everyone had wrong doing in this situation, she had cheated on her husband, and the two of them had cheated. She would never forget but had to let go of the pain. Ebony turned to her sister embracing her.

"Now this is a beautiful sight." Melody stood in the doorway. The two sisters backed away from each other.

"Do we have any wine in this place?"

"You have to ask." Melody walked off into the kitchen. Ebony and India followed her taking a seat on the couch. Ebony grabbed a huge slice of pizza taking a huge bite.

"I have waited months for this."

Melody poured a glass of wine for all three of them passing the glasses around. India took a seat on the carpet and Melody curled up next to her best friend. Ebony curled her legs under her relaxing into the couch. She looked at her best friend thinking how she had missed her. She focused on her sister next. She had missed her too even though some anger was still there. She knew her dad would not have wanted the two of them to be astranged for so long. If losing her dad taught her anything it was that life is short and the people that we cherish the most in our life need to know that. She knew where her next stop would be tomorrow morning.

....

Ebony's eyes popped open as she heard a crash come from the kitchen.

"Sorry, sorry." Melody said as she dropped a frying pan on the kitchen floor. Ebony grabbed her head propping her self up slowly on the couch.

"Want some breakfast?" Ebony opened her eyes up looking over the arm rest of the couch. She saw the clock on the wall.

"You let me sleep until noon?" Melody's head peeked around the corner.

"You were passed out. It's obvious you're exhausted."

She pushed herself up to a seated position rolling her neck to stretch it out. Ebony stood up slowly walking to the bathroom. She jumped in the shower not ready for the day ahead of her but she knew she had to do it.

Thirty minutes later she pulled up to a brick building. She walked in going to the second floor. As she stepped off the elevator, the memories of years of unhappiness flowed back into her body. Day in and day out she sat behind that desk waiting for something to happen to her life and now she was living the dream. It was lonely, but she was on her way to happy.

"Oh my gosh." Jessica jumped out from behind the reception desk running to Ebony. She grabbed her tightly. "It's so good to see you."

"Hi Jess. I see you are holding the fort down."

Jessica tossed her brown hair to the side. "I am. It hasn't been easy but I try."

"Ebony nodded her head knowing that her mother had to have been hard to work for over the last few months.

"Is she in?"

"Yes." Ebony parted from Jess walking towards her mother's closed door. She held her fist up trying to decide if she really wanted to do this or not. She knocked twice before opening the door. Her mother stood with her back to her starring out the window like she always did when deep in thought.

"Yes Jessica."

"It's me mom."

Mrs. Lovely's arms fell to her side. She turned slightly looking at her daughter over her right shoulder.

"Your sister told me you were home. I didn't know if I would see you."

Ebony focused on the ground feeling ashamed. What would her father tell her to do? She hated the distance between her and her mother. It was bearable when her father was alive because he was the middle man, but now it was just them.

Ebony approached her slowly.

"How are you?" Ebony spoke.

"Well, while you are traveling around the country, the rest of us were here working and maintaining."

Ebony scrunched her face. She knew this was a mistake.

"I just wanted to check on you but I see this was a mistake." Ebony turned back towards the door. She grabbed the door knob then stopped. The feud between her and her mother had gone on for too long.

"Why do you hate me so much?" Ebony turned back towards her mother's back. Her eyes filled up with tears. "I'm sorry for whatever I did to you. I wish daddy was still here too, that way you wouldn't have to deal with me, but he's not and I can't change that." She sobbed. "But one day I would like a mother to help me through everything that I am going through as well." Ebony headed for the door again in shock at how she had just spoken to her mother. She felt that might have been the last conversation that they would share so she needed it to count.

Ebony yanked the door open.

"I'm sorry." She stopped. Her mother had never apologized for anything to her. She wiped her tears with both hands.

"Ma'am?" The sides oh her eyes burned as she turned back to face her mother. She hadn't looked her in the eyes in months.

The sun illuminated her mother's outline since she hadn't moved from the window. Ebony shut the door walking slowly towards her mother.

"Your father told me that I needed to support you. Being a singer was never what I wanted for you. A stable, honest career is all I ever asked for you girls. A good education, good job, some grand babies, that was my plan."

"But..." Ebony opened her mouth.

"I'm speaking." She stopped walking letting her mother continue.

"I'm proud of you that you followed your dreams. Even though it's not what I wanted, I want my girls to be happy. This is not what I wanted for me, but it's a good, honest career so that's what I chose." Her mother's voice trembled. Ebony couldn't picture her mother doing anything else. She wondered what her dream had been.

"I saw you on the internet and heard you on the radio." Her voice shook. Ebony took small deep breaths. "I have never been more proud to call you my daughter." Water ran from her mother's eyes. Her daughter joined in as she walked the rest of the way to the window. "I should have been there for you with all the stuff you went through with your husband but I was consumed in my own sorrow. I am so sorry."

Ebony reached out grabbing her mother tightly. The tears wouldn't stop flowing. She had waited her whole life to hear these words from her mother. It was worth the wait.

"Don't be sorry mom. I love you."

"I love you too." Her mother kissed her on the cheek. Ebony pulled back from her laughing. She walked to her mother's desk grabbing a hand full of tissues from off it. She let out a huge sigh. She looked to the sky knowing her dad was smiling down on them.

"The three of us should have dinner tonight."

Ebony shook her head still not being able to speak words. She left the office feeling like anything was possible.

THIRTY-TWO

Ebony ran up the steps to the court house with her best friend trailing behind.

"Slow down, you know I'm a big girl."

"Come on we're late." The ladies ran through the security gate.

"Excuse me ma'am." A tall, chocolate bald headed officer stopped Melody.

"Do you have anything in your pockets, a belt or any jewelry?"

Melody shined her white teeth at him. "You can search me if you'd like." Ebony watched her best friend spread her arms and legs in front of the officer. Ebony rolled her eyes.

"Step to the side ma'am."

Melody stepped out of the way of the incoming traffic. A big female officer walked up to her with a hand held metal detector. Melody's face dropped as she was searched by the less then feminine woman. Ebony laughed hysterically.

"Not funny."

"It really is." Ebony wiped the tears from her eyes.

They made it through security but not without Melody trying to slip the officer her number. They took the elevator up four floors making a right to the first court room on the right. Ebony pushed the door open slowly as they slipped into the back row of the court room. She had been so focused on trying to be on time that she didn't think about facing her husband after months of not seeing him. She looked to her left and saw him sitting all alone.

"Brody vs. Brody?" The judge called.

Ebony and Carson stood.

"Please come forward."

All three of them walked towards the front. They raised their right hands getting sworn in. The judge asked several questions like when they got separated, and had they had sex with each other in the last six months. Then he asked if there was any sign of reconciliation. Ebony turned her head looking at her high school sweetheart. She felt a lump in her throat that she tried to swallow. Carson looked as if he'd lost his best friend. Ebony couldn't bare to look at him and answer the judge at the same time. Everything had happened so fast that she never really thought if they could be together in the future she just knew at this point in time there was no reconciliation. She had forgiven her sister so she felt she had to forgive him too, but forget she couldn't.

"I see no reason not to grant the divorce. If there is no dispute then you should have the final decree in a few weeks." The judge said. The three of them walked out of the court room. Melody walked off to the side as they shut the door to allow Ebony and Carson some private time.

"How are you?" Carson asked.

"I am good. I'm only here for a few days before I go back on tour."

"I'm glad everything is going well. You look well."

Ebony folded her arms. "Thanks."

Her husband grabbed her arms pulling her off to the side sitting on a small white cushion against the wall. She saw the bags forming under his eyes.

"For what it's worth, I am sorry for what happened. I should never have done what I did."

Ebony shook her head. "We both made mistakes. I started this last year. You forgave me for my indiscretions so I feel I have to forgive you, but because it was my sister, it's hard to forget that."

"I understand." Ebony rubbed her hands together trying to absorb the moisture.

"I miss my best friend and my cheerleader."

She chuckled. She missed her friend as well.

"I love you Ebony. I've loved you since we were kids and I will never stop." He grabbed her chin bringing her lips to his. He kissed her deeply.

Ebony squeezed her legs together trying to stop the warm feeling that was between her thighs.

"I love you too." She replied back.

"I will always be there for you, whatever you need. You can always count on me." Ebony starred into his eyes seeing the pain that was in them. Carson was such a good man and she knew he meant every word that he said to her. He had been the love of her life for so long, she didn't know life without him. The couple stood up walking to the elevator hand in hand. Carson pushed the down arrow. Ebony and Melody walked onto the elevator when the door opened. Carson stood back letting her hand slip from his grasp.

"Remember what I said baby. I love you. Good bye Ebony." Carson's eyes filled quickly with tears. It felt like her heart jumped out of her chest. The pain was unbearable. His good bye sounded so final.

"Good bye Carson." She starred into his brown eyes until the double doors blocked her view of him. Her knees buckled and she fell to the floor as soon as he was out of sight. Melody bent down hugging her best friend. Anger had fueled her emotions for the past few months that she never thought about the pain of saying goodbye to her husband. Ebony grabbed her blouse trying to stop the pain coming through her chest. The elevator stopped opening the doors to several on lookers waiting to get onto the elevator. Melody stood up pulling her best friend off the floor. She held on to her for support until they got outside.

"I need a minute." Ebony said as they sat down on the steps to the court house. She closed her eyes inhaling deeply then letting it out slowly trying to contain the tears. Melody put her hand on her best friends shoulder. She pulled her in closely.

"We will get through this together. You know it's not goodbye. The two of you will always be there for each other and you always have me." Ebony grabbed her best friends hand thankful for her. She was also thankful that she would be going back on tour to take her mind of all her pain. Carson came walking out of the courthouse passing them on the steps. He slowed down stopping in front of them. Ebony looked up as the two made eye contact. The side of his mouth turned up. Ebony returned the smile. She gave him a slight head nod. Carson turned his back to her and continued walking. Ebony watched him walk off into the distance. A piece of her heart was walking away. It hurt like hell but she also felt herself become a little lighter. The sun shone on her face and at that moment she felt her father's presence. She closed her eyes turning her face to the sky. Several deep breaths were taken until her breathing slowed down. She rose to her feet walking in the opposite direction of her husband but towards the future that she was always meant to have. No more Jefferson and no more Carson weighing her down. Just her, her voice, and her family finally standing behind her. Ebony felt nothing could stop her.

Printed in the United States
By Bookmasters